REAPER HOUSE

OTHER BOOKS BY
JEFF VANOUDENHOVE

SERIES

THE DARK SERIES

Dark Place
Dark Lane
Dark Queen
Dark Child
The Final Dark

THE ALPHABET KILLER SERIES

The Alphabet Killer
The Letter Man
Killer by Number

STANDALONE NOVELS

Just Listen

Emma

SHORT STORY COLLECTION

Screams in the Dark and Other Twisted Tales

REAPER HOUSE

Jeff VanOudenhove

Westfield, MA

JAVO Publication
Westfield, Massachusetts 01085

This is a work of fiction. The characters, places, and events portrayed in this book are either the product of the author's imagination or are used fictitiously. Any similarity to real persons, living or dead, business establishments, or events is coincidental and not intended by the author.

ISBN: 979-8-9918888-5-1

Library of Congress Control Number: 2025919761

Cover design by Jeff VanOudenhove

For Brittany, Angeline, & Cassandra

Prologue

The house lay dormant for nearly two decades. Its dreary, silent walls remained lifeless and empty after the incident, telling no further tales of the horror that took place beyond the doors on that fateful night, other than the grueling images captured by the crime scene investigators' cameras. What was once a place for devilishly fun, frightful scares during the witching season soon became a house of horrors none would ever forget. On that cold October evening, when monsters lurked around every corner, begging for their treats, another kind of monster was stirring deep in the recesses of Isabelle Unger's soul.

Neither the history books nor the newspaper articles written about the horrific tragedy could tell you what caused Isabelle to snap on that Halloween night in 2009, only that she killed twelve people behind the locked doors of Reaper House.

For thirty-nine years, Reaper House, located on the outskirts of Templeton, Massachusetts, was a favorite attraction for thrill-seekers of everything ghoulish and ghastly during the month of October.

Opened in 1970 by George and Isabelle Unger to a small, local reception of thirteen fervent individuals, a number the married couple considered lucky, the lavish yet eerie haunted house was available for public viewing for only five nights. Though the props were rudimentary and the scares ascetic, with an array of human-like animatronics fashioned to look like butchers and psychotic torturers in a grand production to entertain teenage and adult horror enthusiasts alike, Reaper House became a cherished, unique experience for all visitors. For five years, the Ungers continued tours on the same five-day schedule, opening on October 27th and closing promptly on October 31st at 11:59 pm. The house's popularity soon grew from word of mouth until people traveled from across the state and beyond to enter the haunted halls of the enormous mansion. Beginning in 1976, because of the steady increase in visitors, George and Isabelle decided to increase the number of days Reaper House was open to the public to nine days leading up to Halloween.

The 8,030 square-foot mansion played the largest role, looking like it had been built on a backlot of a large movie studio, ominously overlooking the dirt road from its perch atop a secluded hill, much like Norman Bates' house in the movie Psycho that scared audiences ten years earlier. Each year, the Ungers would add props and animatronics more terrifying than the year before, enthralling newcomers and increasing returning visitors' anticipation.

Throughout Reaper House's history, the Ungers, a known superstitious couple, held onto the belief that thirteen was a lucky number since that was the number of customers they had on their first night. For that reason, only thirteen individuals were allowed entrance into the house at any one time. Only after all thirteen people had exited the premises through the back, where they would weave their way along a path through a spooky cemetery, would the next thirteen be allowed to enter through the front. The tours would take place in twenty-minute intervals, with George and Isabelle rotating shifts during the house's daily operating hours.

By 1992, the haunted house had increased its daily operations to thirteen nights leading up to Halloween. The steady increase in price each year, as well as the growing number of visitors, made it possible for the Ungers to update the mansion further, adding secret passages and hidden rooms to the already exciting tours. But, in 2003, George Unger, at the age of fifty-five, died of respiratory failure due to complications from pneumonia, leaving his widowed Isabelle alone with the burden of maintaining Reaper House.

For six years, Isabelle continued with her and her husband's legacy, though it became harder to keep up with the scheduled tours since she was now alone and growing long in years.

Nobody could know the stresses Isabelle endured after the passing of her husband or what thoughts haunted her dreams each night. But on October 31st, 2009, on a dark and dreary Halloween night, eight teenagers and five adults entered Reaper House for the last time. The doors locked behind them, as they always had, and no more visitors entered after them.

After multiple complaints from waiting parents and customers, which drew the authorities to the property, the doors to Reaper House were forced open, to the sheer horror of the responding officers. The bodies of twelve individuals were found in different rooms of the house in various conditions. Most had been cut or stabbed in one way or another. Two had died from suffocation, with plastic bags still wrapped around their heads. And at least one unlucky visitor had been dismembered, their limbs stacked like firewood in front of the fireplace. It was later reported that authorities believed one victim possibly escaped, since they didn't recover a thirteenth body from inside the house, though it was never confirmed, since the victim never came forward to tell their story.

Isabelle was found sitting in the dark in the mansion's study in a large wingback chair, rocking her upper body back and forth and laughing uncontrollably. She was holding a bloody knife in one hand and a small hatchet in the other, her clothes covered in blood. When the police entered the room where she sat, their flashlights shining on the woman's disturbing appearance, her laughter ceased, and she turned her maniacal stare in their direction.

"The Reaper comes for us all" was heard as an ominous whisper leaving the woman's pale lips before she turned the knife on herself, jamming it into the side of her neck.

Thirteen bodies in all were removed that day. Tainted walls and floors were scrubbed clean of the blood. But the memories of what happened in Reaper House reverberated long after the dead were buried. With no known relatives to claim the property, the mansion was eventually seized and abandoned by the town, left to wither and decay from the effects of time, the dirt access road gated and locked. Reaper House was no more.

Or was it?

Chapter 1

How many people have died where I'm standing, Jamie thought, staring down at the blood-stained floorboards, their warped and unpolished surface showing their decades of use. The open doorway behind her let in enough fading light to showcase the long-dry, crimson pool, but not enough to give her a warm feeling about her decision. The darkened foyer, though empty and spacious, felt constricting with the way the shadows from the tree limbs seemed to creep along the walls, swaying and stretching like octopus arms. Every subtle breeze caused them to quiver, matching the sensation running down Jamie's spine. The late September air was unseasonably warm, but inside, the stale, stagnant atmosphere was biting to her skin and chilled her straight through to her bones. Even her breath dispensed in a plume of condensation with every shallow exhale. The red stain beneath her feet only heightened her sense of dread while her thoughts played horrifying motion pictures in her head about helpless victims meeting their untimely deaths at the hands of a crazed killer. Yet, there she stood, in the same house, on the same spot, wondering if she would share the same fate. And if she should, who would..,

"You know that's just paint, right?" Jamie's best friend, Darlene, stated. She entered behind Jamie, carrying a bag of groceries, her abrupt entrance causing Jamie to jump.

"I know," Jamie replied. She rubbed her palms up and down her arms to dispel the goosebumps her friend had caused. "It looks so real, though."

"Firstly, I'm not going to ask how you would know that," Darlene responded. "And secondly, it had to look real to draw in business. People can tell when something's not legitimate. If the sight of the 'blood' hadn't captured them when they first walked in, the scares throughout the tour wouldn't have been as frightening. Who would have wanted to come back or tell their friends about the place if the whole thing was lame?"

"I guess."

"I can't believe your boss bought this place. Does he know what happened here?"

"Does *anybody* really know what happened here? Anyway, yes. The realtor informed him about the deaths."

"The murders, you mean," Darlene corrected her friend.

"Same difference."

"Girl, that's *different* difference."

Jamie rolled her eyes.

"Remind me again why we had to stay here tonight," Darlene questioned.

"Because *you* didn't want to wake up at the butt-crack of dawn tomorrow morning to drive three hours to get here, remember?"

"No, I get that. But why are we staying *here* when there's a perfectly good hotel only a few miles up the road?"

"I'm not paying two hundred dollars a night when we have a fully furnished house to stay in for free."

"Free to die in, too, from the look of it."

"Oh, stop it."

The shuffling sound of footsteps behind the two women alerted them to the arrival of a third in their group.

"What are you guys just standing there for?" Vickie questioned, peering over their shoulders to see if something had impeded their path. "These bags aren't getting any lighter."

"Oh, sorry," Jamie said. She turned and stepped to the side to allow entrance into the foyer. "I can take one of those for you."

Jamie outstretched her arm, offering to relieve her friend of one of the large, reusable grocery bags, but the tall, lanky woman shot her an unaccepting glance.

"I didn't say I was weak," Vickie griped. She furrowed her brow while pulling the bags tighter to her sides.

"Okay, sorry," Jamie spat sarcastically, putting her hands up in front of her chest and rolling her eyes. "*You* struggle with them, then."

Jamie didn't take offense. She knew Vickie was still dealing with hormonal changes during her transition and the gradual muscle loss due to the estrogen treatments. Though her friend had been through therapy for years, preparing for her lifestyle change, Jamie didn't think Vickie had been fully aware of the kind of emotional toll the changes to her body would place upon her mind. But her friends all supported her and would continue to do so, even if her attitude became brusque at times.

"Where's Samara?" Jamie asked while peeking out the front door.

"She's on the phone with Chuck," Vickie answered. She walked by the other two girls in search of a light switch.

"Barf," Darlene added. She let her tongue roll out of her mouth like she was gagging. "I don't know what she sees in that guy." She walked to a staircase along the right wall and draped the loops of the grocery bags she was carrying over the ornate newel post. "She can do so much better."

"Stop it," Jamie said. "He's not that bad. Besides, we've all fallen for Mister Wrong at some point."

"Ah ha!" Darlene stated with exuberance. "So you *do* think he's no good."

"I didn't say that."

Vickie, using her left elbow to flip a light switch on the wall while looking up at the gaudy, unresponsive chandelier, spoke up.

"You literally just implied it."

"What? No, I didn't."

"Yes, you did," Darlene replied, softly snickering.

"Well, I didn't mean it that way."

"You still said it," Darlene continued. She smirked triumphantly.

"What*ever*," Vickie said with a huff. "Can someone just please point me in the direction of the kitchen? These bags are heavy."

"I think it might be that doorway straight ahead." Jamie pointed out a barely visible archway down a narrow corridor to the left of the staircase.

"Then, that's where I'm going," Vickie replied. She sauntered forward into the darkened hallway. "Lights aren't working, by the way," she added over her shoulder as she fell out of sight.

Darlene shook her head, exhaling heavily. "That one's going to be a handful."

"We agreed we'd stay positive - that we wouldn't let her get on our nerves."

"Fine," Darlene shrugged. "I can handle it if you can. It's just..," her voice trailed off.

"What?" Jamie questioned, though she already knew her friend's response.

"Remember what happened last time?" She raised her eyebrows to make a statement. "I'm going out to grab the rest of the bags."

Darlene walked by Jamie, giving her a side-eyed glare as if to say, *I'm not going through that again*. Jamie didn't need the subtle reminder of the past. She was well aware of Vickie's past uncontrollable anger. But that was before her treatments. The new Vickie wasn't anything like her former self.

She shook her head, letting out a frustrated breath from her nose and watching the vapor release like a broken steam pipe. Seeing her breath caused her to shiver as goosebumps once again formed on her skin. Shaking off the cold, she looked at the walls on either side of her, the lower halves covered in dark brown stained wainscoting panels. The upper walls, separated from the wainscoting by a chair rail that ran along the top of the panels, were decorated with a heavy-textured, densely patterned, blueish wallpaper that had a foil inlay that shimmered faintly in the dim light sneaking in from the front door. Both side walls showcased open-arched doorways leading into other rooms. Choosing the left wall, Jamie made her way to the opening and looked into the darkness. Outside the entryway, she couldn't help but instinctively flip the same light switch Vickie had tried moments before as if her touch would somehow miraculously produce different results. She knew the electric company wasn't coming out until the following morning, but an innate desire to see where she was going was a difficult habit to break.

Realizing she'd forgotten the flashlight in the front seat of her car, she pulled out her cell phone to improvise and noticed a text on her screen that had come through ten minutes earlier.

Stopped for beer. Almost there.

It was from her on-again/off-again boyfriend, Pierce. At the moment, they were in their off-again stage, choosing to remain friendly until one of them decided it was time to be on-again. Still, she hadn't asked him to come, but his best friend Chuck took it upon himself to invite Pierce along. Chuck hadn't been invited, either, but Samara begged him to come. It didn't matter. Whatever her feelings, she knew how to play it cool.

She clicked on the flashlight on her phone and pointed it into the room, hoping she'd avoid the sight of creepy-crawly insects or hairy rodents scurrying for cover in tiny crevices in the walls. That would put an end to any idea she might have had about getting sleep. Thankfully, everything seemed clear and unmoving within the beam of her phone's light. She let out a breath of relief and felt her tensed shoulders instantly relax. *One less thing to worry about*, she thought.

Barely a foot within the dark room, Jamie quickly swept the light from left to right to gather a sense of her surroundings before taking another step. The room appeared fully furnished and was so large that her light couldn't penetrate enough of the darkness to reach the far wall. The already cold air felt somehow colder in that room. Frozen in place and staring straight ahead, trying to focus her vision and hoping it would soon acclimate to her black surroundings, she felt the hair on her arms stand at attention as if they knew something she didn't. Just then, she heard a creaking sound in the far right corner, which sent a chill down her spine and numbed her limbs. Feeling panicky, she flashed the light in that direction but couldn't see anything farther than an old-style, wingback chair situated in the center of the floor. Her chest tightened, and her breath became shallow. Deciding discretion was the better part of valor, she immediately attempted to exit the room, but as she turned, she collided with a figure standing in her way. Jamie let out a blood-curdling scream before falling backward to the ground.

Chapter 2

The ensuing laughter Jamie heard was both degrading and soothing. She looked up at Pierce and Chuck, covering their mouths in hysterics, and felt her heart rate beginning to slow back down to a normal pace. The embarrassment and frustration quickly faded, as did the pale hue from her cheeks. She felt oddly safer now. The rest of her friends had arrived.

Jamie picked herself up and unsteadily made her way to the base of the stairs. She sat on the second step, tapping her foot in annoyance, listening to Chuck and Pierce go on with their childish banter.

"You should have seen your face," Chuck stated excitedly, holding back a snicker.

"It *was* pretty funny, wasn't it?" Pierce added, rapping his friend's upper arm with a light fist.

Seeing the two of them act in such a way made Jamie wonder why she had ever started dating Pierce in the first place.

"Are you guys done?" Jamie asked, crossing her arms in front of her chest, conveying her aggravation.

"Yeah, I suppose we're through," Chuck answered.

Jamie shifted her eyes back and forth between the two men angrily before smiling and extending her arms.

"Good. Now help me up."

As they lifted her to her feet, she snuggled herself between them, hugging them simultaneously.

"Thanks for coming, guys. It will make this whole thing easier."

She relaxed her grip from around Chuck but held Pierce a little longer than she should have, breathing in his cologne. She couldn't help but notice it was the same brand she'd bought him on their trip to Maine together. The memory of that weekend made her wonder why she'd ever broken up with him.

She snapped to her senses and peeled herself away from her ex, realizing where her dangerous thoughts could lead. "Anyway, I wasn't scared; you just surprised me."

Pierce smiled and gave her a wink. "I know."

"Seriously, though," Jamie reiterated louder, addressing all of her friends who were now gathered in the foyer, "I appreciate all of you guys for coming out here. If I had to do this myself, it'd take a week."

"It still may," Vickie stated, looking around at whatever was still visible in the fading light, her upper lip curled in a sneer.

"Don't listen to Vic," Chuck said. "We're happy to help."

"Only because you haven't seen the kitchen yet," Vickie grumbled under her breath.

Even so, Jamie gave Chuck a cynical stare as if she couldn't believe what she'd just heard. For one, it wasn't like Chuck to be so polite and agreeable to anything she said, and two, well.., that was all she could come up with. See example number one.

"Besides," Chuck continued, "think of the awesome party we're going to have in this place."

And there it was, she thought. *There's always an ulterior motive with that one.*

"No, nope," Jamie said, wagging her finger. "No parties."

"Aw, come on," Chuck griped. "Maybe just a little one?"

Darlene jumped in, "It wouldn't be a horrible idea, Jamie. I mean.., look at this place. When would you ever get another opportunity to have a party in a freaking mansion?"

Jamie rolled her eyes, knowing full well that Darlene was pouring it on thick. Still, she wasn't wrong. And her friends *were* gracious enough to agree to help her out. Perhaps a little "thank you" party wouldn't be such a bad thing, as long as her boss didn't find out.

Raymond Blanchard, owner of Blanchard Realty Investments, bought the property, sight unseen, for a steal. It came with a stipulation from the town written into the contract that the *"house could not be used or operated in any manner as to suggest the property and/or all structures thereon might be haunted, or in a fashion that would convey a sense of overwhelming fear or general unease to the community."* It was an odd stipulation, and one she wasn't sure was entirely legal, but that was fine for Raymond, whose sole interest in the property was to update the structure and flip it for a profit. He was going to be out of town for a few weeks, visiting other properties he'd invested in that were in various states of reconstruction. He asked Jamie, his number two, to go to the once-infamous Reaper House estate and take detailed notes of the mansion's interior, room by room, so he could get a better understanding of the scope of work that would need to take place.

"Okay, fine," Jamie acquiesced to her friends. "But only *after* I see you guys are taking this seriously. With eight of us, we should be able to finish up before the weekend is through. The Electric Company is coming tomorrow morning to replace the meter and turn on the power; that gives us two days. If we get the majority of the house inspected tomorrow morning and afternoon, we can have your little party tomorrow night. Then, we finish on Sunday and go home."

"Anything else, Warden?" Vickie commented.

Jamie ignored her friend's comment as much as possible, but still let out a frustrated huff from her nose. Then, she lit up with an effervescent smile and began clapping her hands excitedly like she was still in high school.

"This is going to be so great, guys. I can't believe you all made it." She flashed a heartfelt glare at all in attendance.

Darlene Blaise, her best friend since seventh grade, who always joked about being the whitest black girl in Templeton, rode up with her on the drive. Vickie and Samara arrived right behind them in Samara's Mini Cooper, which Jamie assumed was what started Vickie on her negative attitude slide.

Vickie DeStello always looked awkward among her peers, with her thin frame and her lanky arms and legs. At six feet, three inches tall, she stood several inches above most of the boys in school. In the whole town, really. Though she felt more comfortable in her body now that she had transitioned, her height and lankiness made her look even more awkward as a female. With her long legs, it couldn't have been a comfortable commute in Samara's Mini.

On the other hand, Samara Ludendorff melted perfectly into her tiny vehicle. Barely exceeding the five-foot benchmark, if it wasn't for her out-of-date '80s permed hairstyle standing on end, you could barely see her over the steering wheel. She was a lovely woman – an absolute joy to be around. It was for that reason her friends were so perplexed when they learned she'd started dating Chuck.

It wasn't that Chuck Weaver was a horrible guy, mainly because the term "guy" usually defined someone who acted more like an adult than a child. Chuck never quite made it past his pubescent phase, joking around all the time and playing pranks on everyone like he was still the class clown. Ten years out of high school, and he still hadn't matured. Jamie figured it might have something to do with his insecurities. He was handsome, but never believed it himself, always rejecting compliments as if people were lying to him. He'd never liked his naturally curly hair and thought he had to be overly funny to take others' attention away from it. He probably took it too far, and he kept up with it longer than he should have.

Pierce Gagnon, on the other hand, knew how to be serious, but his maturity seemed to go by the wayside whenever Chuck was around. Jamie couldn't stand to be around him when he acted like an imbecile, feeding into Chuck's warped sense of humor. But when he was the guy she fell in love with, he made her feel like she was the only woman around. She missed that feeling. She missed the way his arms wrapped around her like a warm blanket. She could have let the world pass by around them to stay in those moments forever. But their relationship faltered, and she found herself longing for what they once shared. Still, every time she looked at his perfect face with his perfectly gelled black hair, and his dazzling blue eyes, and his inviting smile with sparkling white teeth, and his..,

She realized she'd gotten lost in her thoughts for a moment and dialed them back in to her current reality.

Shawn Higgins was a late addition to the group. He'd heard about the trip from Chuck and asked if he could tag along. Chuck gave his approval as if it were his to give. The problem was, it wasn't. Jamie hadn't learned of Shawn's invitation until he was already well en route and couldn't bring herself to ask him to turn back. It wasn't that she didn't appreciate the help, but Shawn was somewhat of a slob. He weighed over 350 lbs and waddled when he walked. His beard and mustache were always unkempt, and his clothes had more food stains than a restaurant tablecloth after dinner. The man sweated profusely, and he reeked of body odor. Honestly, Jamie didn't know how much he'd be able to contribute or how much she'd be able to stand being around him.

And then there was Brandon Landon, destined from birth to be the butt of all jokes the moment his parents named him. To ensure he would never overcome such overwhelming humiliation, Brandon fashioned a fancy set of buck teeth and a lazy left eye that often veered in the opposite direction as his right. Jamie didn't know who invited him or how he ended up at Reaper House, but he was there, and she'd do her best to make him feel welcome.

"Well, guys," Jamie began, "the sun's going down quickly, and it's getting dark in here. I suggest we roll out our sleeping bags and blankets in one of these downstairs rooms until tomorrow. In the morning, when we can see where we're going, we can check out the rest of the house and choose our bedrooms. Everybody okay with that?"

"Do we have a choice?" Vickie spoke up.

"Not unless you want to go back into town and pay for a hotel room."

"Then, I guess, our blankets it is."

"Great!" Jamie said enthusiastically. "This is going to be one hell of an awesome weekend."

Chapter 3

Jamie awoke from her slumber; her eyes thrust open to the sound of old floorboards creaking. Her chest tightened as she stared helplessly into the darkness, the whirring hum of Shawn's CPAP machine trying strenuously to disguise the creepy noises of an old house's aging bones. Her head remained sunken in the comfort of her feathery pillow while her eyes darted in all directions, seeking out any source of light that would calm her nerves. Her ears were on full alert, listening to the heavy breathing of her sleeping housemates and the pounding of her heart against her ribs. The wind began to howl outside the large, picturesque window along the front wall, its view letting in no more of the moon's brilliance than the remaining solid walls that surrounded her. A sudden sensation along her forearm made her flail her arm wildly. Then she realized it wasn't an insect that had crept onto her, but her own skin that was crawling. That freaked her out even more.

She felt her heartbeat increase as she listened intently for another out-of-place sound. As she tried to shift her body, her legs wouldn't move, pinned to the floor by some unknown weight. She slid her hand across the floor, feeling for her phone, which she remembered placing by her head before drifting off. When she found it, she nervously faced it toward her legs, her hand shaking. She clicked on the flashlight and immediately stiffened, having thought the worst and preparing for whatever was about to jump at her. At the sight, her shoulders relaxed in relief as she let out a held breath. Darlene had fallen asleep perpendicular to her, using Jamie's calf as a pillow. Jamie quietly chuckled, shaking her head at her ridiculous thoughts.

"What were you expecting it to be?" she whispered to herself. With the light still on, Jamie slowly swung her outstretched arm in a swath around her to check on her other friends. Vickie had taken up residence on the floral-patterned sofa. *Of course*, Jamie thought. *She's too much of a diva to be caught dead on the floor.* Continuing the phone's travel, Chuck was asleep in an upright position on the large wingback chair, his right leg flopped over the chair's arm. Samara was sprawled out in front of the chair by his left foot. *What a gentleman Chuck is, claiming the chair for himself instead of for his girlfriend. Though she probably lucked out. There's no telling what kind of bugs or rodents laid claim to the furniture before we got here.*

Jamie went to swing the phone further when another creaking sound, louder than the first, erupted from the hall outside the room's arched entryway. Her hand darted toward the opening, the lit phone exposing only dust particles fluttering about in the light's beam. She felt her chest tighten again as a second floorboard creaked from out of sight in the hallway. Her ears then picked up on a scraping sound along the wall just beyond the corner. She shook her leg in an attempt to wake her friend, but Darlene remained asleep, simply mumbling, "Not yet; another hour." Her friend did, however, readjust her head to a pillow located in the bend of Jamie's knees, freeing Jamie of the dead weight that was holding her down.

Jamie flipped the blanket off herself and rotated her body into a kneeling position, the light from her phone held fast on the doorway. In the next moment, time seemed to stand still as a set of pale fingers slowly came into view, wrapping around the doorframe. Her eyes widened, and she took in a quivering breath, ready to let out a scream for help, but before she could, a bright light shone in her eyes, blinding her and causing her to reel. She let out a different scream while throwing her hand up in front of her eyes to block the light.

"Ow!"

"Oh, sorry," a faint voice whispered, trying to keep quiet, though it was now unnecessary.

Jamie's scream had awoken all in the room except Shawn, whose humming machine, kept powered by his battery backup, left him favorably unconscious.

"What the hell, Jamie?" Chuck spoke, swinging his right leg off the chair's arm to meet his left leg and kicking Samara's hip in the process.

"Hey, watch it!"

"Sorry, babe."

"Jamie, what is it? What's going on?" Darlene asked as a slew of phones lit up like a spotlight focused on their friend.

"Just..," she pointed forward, "just him."

In unison, all the lights shifted to the doorway, aiming at the figure under the arch, who averted his eyes.

Pierce raised his voice, "Brandon! What the fuck, man? What are you doing, creeping around?"

"I had to go to the bathroom."

"What was that scraping sound I heard?" Jamie asked.

"That was me, sliding my hand along the wall to find my way back. It's not easy finding your way around in the dark."

"What do you mean?" Jamie questioned. "You have your phone."

"My phone stopped working when I got into the hall," Brandon answered. "It's weird; it just came back on as I entered this room."

"Shut up, Brandon," Chuck said. "That's stupid."

"It's true. Watch; I'll show you."

Brandon stepped back into the hall, expecting his phone to go dead, but it remained functional.

"What the hell?" He shook his phone as if trying to get it to stop working.

"Good one, Brandon," Pierce said sarcastically. "And for your next trick..,"

"I swear, guys. It wasn't working a moment ago."

"Yeah, okay," Chuck blurted, rolling his eyes. "The guy doesn't even know how to use his phone."

Samara slapped Chuck's leg. "Stop it, Chuck. Be nice."

Vickie jumped in, "You probably just accidentally turned the flashlight off with your finger and didn't realize it."

"But.., but I didn't."

"Whatever," Vickie added. "Can we just go back to sleep now?"

"I'm down for that," Chuck answered as he turned his light off and rolled over in the chair.

Brandon looked sorrowful and said in a timid voice, "I'm sorry, Jamie," as he stepped over Darlene on the way to his vacant blanket. "I didn't mean to scare you."

"It's okay, Brandon," she replied. "It's not you. It's this house. It'll be less creepy when we have power."

Darlene huffed aggravatingly. "Yeah, we don't all have the luxury of a battery backup like Shawn's CPAP," she stated, wondering how he could sleep through all the noise and also wondering how she was going to get back to sleep, herself, hearing its whirring motor.

"Sorry, everyone," Jamie said sympathetically. "I'll make it up to you by cooking breakfast in the morning."

"You mean, assuming the power company comes early enough," Darlene added.

"Right," Jamie agreed.

"That's only a good apology if we all manage to wake up before Shawn," Pierce said. "Otherwise, there won't be anything left."

Jamie rolled her eyes, choosing not to respond to his comment. One by one, the phone lights turned off. Jamie slid back down onto her side and rested her head on her soft pillow. She maintained her open-eyed stare into the darkness as long as she could until exhaustion overtook her, and she drifted off.

Chapter 4

Jamie pulled the curtain aside to check on the worker's progress as he installed an updated meter on the side of the house. She had awoken just past eight o'clock and began detailing notes about the mansion's library when, about a half hour later, she heard the vehicle's tires crunching along the gravel driveway. She'd stepped onto the front porch to greet the worker as he exited his truck. He introduced himself as Dave from the power company and proceeded to pull a small metallic box from the passenger seat. When asked where he could find the meter, Jamie shrugged. "I have no idea. I just got here late last night." His response didn't give her a warm feeling inside.

"You stayed overnight? In this house? Without any power? That's brave of you. Especially after what happened to those two boys a few years back."

"What do you mean?" Jamie asked. "What boys? What happened?"

"You're not from around here, are you?" Dave responded.

Jamie shook her head. "I'm from New York."

"You know about this place, right?" he asked, pointing his finger to the upper floors and shifting his eyes from side to side like he was studying each of the windows, expecting someone to be staring back at him.

"Yeah. Reaper House," Jamie answered. "An old Halloween attraction. I'd never been here, though. I was still young when the place closed down. My parents weren't the type to drive a few hours to bring their daughter to a haunted house."

"You're probably lucky for that," the man replied, "it could have been you that night."

Jamie forced a grin at the uncomfortable comment. It was bad enough that staying in Reaper House was unsettling; she didn't need the horrible reminder of what happened to Isabelle Unger's victims. Still, she was curious about his earlier comment about the two boys.

"You mentioned something about a couple of boys?" she questioned.

"Oh yeah," the worker nodded, scratching the stubble on his chin with his finger. "The story wasn't publicized much. Not with the history of this place being a blight on Templeton. I think the town wanted to shut the story down as quickly as they could. It was a shame, though. Brothers. Thomas and Rory Wilkinson. They broke into the place to see if there was anything worth stealing. That's what the news reported, anyway. The older boy, Thomas - he was fifteen - his body was found out back in the tall grass beyond the makeshift graveyard. He was cut up pretty badly, eventually succumbing to his wounds. Rumor has it he was purposely left there to die. The thirteen-year-old, Rory, was found hanging from some light fixture in the entryway."

Jamie's thoughts immediately snapped to the large chandelier in the foyer.

"The kid had a note stuck to him by a knife that had been plunged into his chest. It said, 'The reaper made me do it.'"

Jamie gasped. "That's awful. So, what, some-one was in the house and killed them?"

"That's what *I* think," Dave stated. "The police wrote it up as a murder/suicide."

"Really? What, did they think the older boy stabbed and hanged his younger brother? How would he even get him up there? Or did the young-er brother cut his older brother and then hang himself? But then, how would he have stabbed himself in the chest? That's all just too weird for me to think about."

"Tell me about it," the man responded. "Anyway, sorry; I didn't mean to cause you any alarm. I was just surprised when I saw the address on my dispatch. I didn't realize anyone would actually purchase this place. Either way, I'll take a look around the property and see if I can locate the meter. I'll have the power on for you in a jiff."

"Thank you."

Twenty minutes had passed since that initial encounter, and he was still finagling with tangled wires sprouting from the mansion's exterior façade and the unruly vines that had crept up the wooden shakes and engulfed the original electrical meter. Jamie began to wonder what "jiff" meant in this backwater town, or if the power would even work in this old, creepy house. Before she could ponder it further, a hand grabbed her right shoulder, causing her to jump and her left elbow to bang against the window as she turned.

"Hey, relax, girl," Darlene said. "It's me." She glanced over Jamie's shoulder out the window to see what had her friend's attention. Dave had heard the thud on the window and was staring back at her. "Is that the guy from the electric company?" she asked. "He's cute."

"Yeah. Don't get any ideas. He's off limits."

"What? You asked?"

"No! Of course not. But he's wearing a ring."

"Ah ha!" Darlene blurted. "So you looked."

"Shh; he's right there." Jamie threw her thumb over her shoulder.

Darlene took another peek out the window. The electrician smiled and nodded, throwing his hand up in a nonchalant wave. Darlene returned a smile, then backed away from the window out of his line of sight and pulled Jamie with her.

"Enough of that guy," Darlene said, flopping her hand over in his direction as if he were already old news. "What about Pierce?"

Jamie's brow furrowed. "What about him?"

"Oh, come on. You don't think I can't see the subtle glances and the playful smiles between you two?"

"Oh my God, Darlene, shut up. We're just friends now."

"Uh-huh; sure." Darlene winked.

"It's true. We had our chance, and it didn't work out. I'm perfectly fine with that. I think we're better off as just friends."

Darlene grinned and nodded skeptically. "Of course, it doesn't hurt that there's a good-looking guy right outside that window."

Just then, the lights in the library flickered on and off a couple of times before finally illuminating the room. Jamie looked up at the overhead light fixture, then back at her friend and smiled.

"Doesn't hurt." She raised and lowered her eyebrows in a teasing manner. "Now go wake the others, and I'll get breakfast started."

Darlene snapped her fingers as she turned to leave the library. "Knew it, ho."

Jamie held in a snicker and shook her head. She appreciated that she and her friend could razz each other as they often did. She took in a deep breath and let it out, relieved that the house now had power. She looked around the room. With the lights on, it seemed less eerie. Ordinary, even. Just a lot of dust and cobwebs to clean. There wasn't anything remotely scary about it, and she wondered how she got herself so worked up over the place just because there were no lights. There wasn't anything to be worried about.

She was about to walk away to begin preparing food when she heard a voice coming from the window. When she looked out, Dave was facing toward the rear of the house, speaking with somebody, and motioning with his hands. She turned her stare further to the left to see with whom he was speaking, but there was nobody there. Her eyes shifted back to the worker, while he continued his conversation. She tried listening, but through the window, his speech was garbled and unintelligible. She looked to the rear of the house again, and still, nobody. Then, the man suddenly stopped talking and slowly turned his head to her. His delightful smile was absent, as was any sign of life in his cold stare. Then, he turned and made his way around the front corner of the house toward the driveway and out of sight from her view.

That was strange, Jamie thought. *Oh yeah. Nothing to be worried about at all. Just the crazy, hot guy lunatic working outside.* She made herself chuckle to calm her nerves. She reached for the curtain and pulled it aside, taking a final glance toward where the worker was speaking. Still seeing nobody present, her thoughts shifted to the unpleasant stare he gave her before walking away. She realized no amount of chuckling would help.

Chapter 5

The driver pulled away before Jamie could even get back to the front door to thank him. As she watched the back of his truck disappear after turning around a sharp bend in the driveway, she stepped down the stairs of the porch and looked toward the corner of the house in curiosity. She swore the worker was talking to somebody on the side of the house. Convincing herself that a short walk in that direction would be to check his work rather than to curb her inquisitiveness (that's what she told herself, anyway), she strolled to the side of the mansion to peek around the corner. Had it been nighttime, a simple task like that would have been out of the question. In the daylight hours, however, with the sun peering over the evergreens that bordered the property, the mansion looked no more intimidating than the museums she visited on her trip to Washington, DC.

Even without the thought of any possible danger, Jamie took a wide berth when she neared the corner of the building. If anyone were to jump out at her, she wanted to give herself enough space to see them coming. When she peered past the corner, it was just as she suspected; there was nobody there and no cause for alarm. She continued traveling along the side of the house on her way to the backyard, stopping once to glance at the newly installed meter, and then up at the window above it, from where she had witnessed the electrician having a one-sided conversation. She rolled her eyes and continued walking, having remembered that Dave mentioned a graveyard of sorts in the backyard. She imagined it was for aesthetics to make the haunted mansion appear more terrifying.

When she arrived at the rear corner of the large dwelling, she was shocked to see how elaborate the "makeshift" graveyard, as Dave called it, was. There were at least a dozen headstones that appeared authentic, located sporadically across the lawn. Her wandering thoughts ridiculously landed on the story of the twelve victims killed within Reaper House. It would have been wild, if not disturbing, had their bodies been put to rest on the very property where they were murdered.

Jamie's eyes shot beyond the graveyard to the tall grass in the field. Dave told her the tragic story of the two boys. Thomas Wilkinson, the older brother, was found out there. Somewhere. She wondered how long he lay there suffering before he died. How long before anyone came to retrieve his body? It was a sad story, one she didn't want to linger on. She let out a weighty breath and rubbed the goosebumps back into her arms.

With heavy steps and a heavier heart, she made her way back to the front of the mansion to carry on with the rest of her day. When she opened the front door, the smell of bacon and freshly brewed coffee, mixed with a musty, mildewy odor, engulfed her senses.

"Shit! Breakfast," she whispered.

She closed the door behind her and froze for a moment to stare up at the chandelier where thirteen-year-old Rory Wilkinson's body once hung. Other children had died in Reaper House - seven or eight, if she remembered the story correctly - but she knew none of the details of those others. Hearing of Rory and Thomas, though, affected her more deeply than she realized.

The sound of laughter coming from the kitchen broke her out of her morbid thoughts. She painted on a smile and trekked past the hallway staircase toward the cheerful banter.

"Hey, guys," she said with guilt in her voice. "I'm sorry I didn't get breakfast started for you."

"It's fine, Jamie," Chuck announced. "Darlene told us all about the stud you were distracted by."

Jamie's eyes instinctively shot toward Pierce, worried about an unpleasant reaction. "What? No. That wasn't it at all."

"Relax, Jamie," Vickie said. "We all know Darlene is full of shit."

Darlene pointed the spatula she was using to flip eggs. "That's it; no more eggs for you."

Shawn took that opportunity to jump in, raising his arm enthusiastically, "I'll take them."

"You *would*, Shawn," Chuck responded, behind a slight chuckle.

"What?" Shawn replied, shrugging his shoulders. "She's been cut off."

Samara groaned. "She was joking, Shawn."

"Well, I didn't know."

Darlene shook her head and looked in Jamie's direction. "You want some eggs and bacon? We have bread, too. Brandon brought a toaster."

"No thanks," Jamie replied sullenly. "I'll just make myself a coffee."

Pierce got up from the crowded table and slid next to Jamie while she poured herself a cup.

"Everything okay?" he asked. "You seem preoccupied."

Jamie didn't want to explain what she'd learned about the brothers' deaths. She didn't want her needless worries passed on to her friends. She opted to keep it generic, and about the story they already knew.

"I think it just hit me this morning," she began. "Thirteen people died in this house, twelve of them killed by a crazed woman. Most of them were kids. It's sad, you know? What the poor parents must have gone through."

"Hey, hey," Pierce offered in a sympathetic tone, pulling Jamie into a gentle embrace. "It *is* sad, but it was a long time ago. And think positively. Now the place will be renovated and sold to a family that can start a brand new life. It will be a happy ending."

From the table, Chuck couldn't help but add his own spin on the dour conversation. "Plus, the old hag that lived here killed *herself*, too, so she got what she deserved."

Samara slapped Chuck's leg under the table. "Jesus, Chuck. Can't you ever be serious?"

"I *was* serious!" he exclaimed. "I mean, after killing all those people.., shit, she was probably going to fry anyway. The way I see it, she saved the taxpayers a whole lot of money by offing herself."

Having heard enough, Jamie set her cup down on the counter, noticeably distraught.

"Enjoy your breakfast, guys," she said in the nicest (fakest) tone possible while forcing a smile. "I'm going to find a bathroom and take a quick shower."

"Oh, hell yes," Vickie added, snapping a finger in the air. "A place this size is going to have multiple bathrooms. I'm going to find one, too, and wash the creepiness off me."

Jamie stopped at the kitchen threshold and addressed the group. "Do what you gotta do: wash up, find a room, unpack your stuff. Let's all meet back down here in the study for 11:00 so I can go over what we're doing. I want to get this done before the weekend is over."

She turned to walk away, but stopped herself. Looking over her shoulder without turning to face them, she smiled to let them know she wasn't as upset as she might have come across. "Guys, we're going to have fun. You'll see."

Chapter 6

The water was hot and just what Jamie needed. It washed away her melancholy disposition, if not her questions about the electrician's unusual behavior. She brushed it off, settling on the notion that he was talking to himself. It no longer mattered. There was power, and there was hot water. That was all she needed to ensure the rest of her weekend was productive.

She stepped from the shower and wrapped the towel she'd placed on the double vanity around herself. The bathroom she'd found was on the second floor at the top of the staircase on the right-hand side. It was smaller than she thought it would be, given the size of the house, but plenty large enough for her needs. She surmised the others would have better luck finding the larger bathrooms, especially Vicki, who probably scoured the place until she found one that met her palatial tastes. Still, the one Jamie found was practically immaculate compared to the bathroom at the last place in which she stayed. There was some mildew she had to wipe away from the shower walls, but this one didn't have oil-stained handprints on the porcelain sink or moldy grout in the tilework surrounding the shower. She'd call that a win.

She grabbed her underwear from the top of the stack of clothes she'd brought in with her and slid them on under the towel while she admired the bathroom's accents and appearance.

The walls were covered from floor to ceiling with what used to be white vertical tiles that had since yellowed, with a light gray pattern that looked like swirling smoke off the end of a lit cigarette. The double vanity was about six feet in length and had two square-shaped, polished white sinks sunken into a darker, solid-gray granite countertop that rested on dust-covered, painted white cabinetry. The sink's fixtures were nickel-plated and shaped like spouts you'd see on an old-style well, each having only a single lever at the top, fashioned to look like well pumps, to control the water temperature. The mirror above, now clouded over with condensation that showed speckles of black grit covering its surface, spanned the distance of the vanity, its bottom edge sitting atop a tiled splash guard, and its top edge meeting the ceiling. To the left of the vanity, the room's toilet was oval-shaped with an oval tank on top, and was the same dark gray color as the vanity. It didn't have a lever for flushing, but instead, a round push-button on the tank's cover. There was no tub in this particular bathroom, only a glass-enclosed shower with a large, square showerhead hung from the ceiling to simulate falling rain. It had everything she wished she'd had in her own bathroom, except for a soaker tub, which she was sure she'd find elsewhere in the estate.

She grabbed her little mesh toiletry bag containing her personal necessities from beside her clothes and slid it toward her. She sifted through it, feverishly looking for a hairbrush to begin her morning beautification ritual. When she couldn't find it, she recalled that she'd taken it out the morning before and placed it on the bedroom bureau in her apartment to allow for her toothbrush and toothpaste. She must have forgotten to repack the brush.

"Shit!" she let out. She huffed in frustration and dropped her chin to her chest. "Okay, no big deal," she whispered. "Darlene will let me use hers." Of course, that meant wandering through the mansion with her hair in its current state, looking for wherever Darlene might have found herself. *How bad could it be*, she thought.

She looked up at the foggy mirror and then at the ceiling, just then realizing there was no vent fan to help control the lingering steam. She placed her right palm on the glass in front of her left shoulder and gave a quick arcing swipe toward the right to rid the glass of clinging moisture and grime. In that moment, her blood froze, and her heart jumped into her throat, constricting her ability to breathe. In the mirror's reflection, over Jamie's left shoulder, stood a boy, maybe fifteen years old, staring at her through blank eyes. He had messy, dark-brown hair, and his complexion was pale white to match the porcelain sinks. His cheeks were hollow, and his lips were puffy and purple.

Jamie stiffened and audibly gasped. Her arm flailed wildly, hitting her toiletry bag and spilling its contents onto the floor. She twisted in place, flinging her backside against the hard, granite vanity to face the boy, but he wasn't there. The room was empty, save for her and the shed skin she jumped out of.

"What the fuck?" she questioned aloud, breathing heavily as she placed her right hand on her chest to quell her nerves. She could feel her hand trembling through the towel. She shifted her eyes left, then right, then straight ahead. She swallowed hard, licking her dry lips, trying to control her breathing and bring herself back to reality.

There was nobody there, she thought, reasoning with herself. *It was all in my head. I just imagined it. Fuck! This place is getting to me.*

She closed her eyes and let out a heavy breath. When she opened them, a thought sprang into her head. She didn't know why, but something gripped her and twisted her insides until she felt nauseous. Her breath became shallow once again as she slowly, nervously turned her head over her right shoulder to get another glimpse in the mirror. With her heart beating through her chest, her eyes methodically scanned past the shower door, the toilet, the edge of the mirror, until finally landing on the smeared streak displaying an image of her frightened face. Nothing else. She felt her shoulders drop two inches in relief, and her chest loosened.

She leaned forward, slumping her body and pressing her palms into the granite top to support herself. With her head down in defeat, her eyes caught sight of the mess she'd made on the floor, and she shook her head, deflated. She brought her hand up to wipe her face of the liquid that had formed, and she wondered if it was nervous sweat or from the steam sticking to her skin. It didn't matter. She quickly grabbed her clothes, pressing them against the front of her towel, and reached for the door. She no longer cared what her hair looked like; she wanted out of that bathroom. She'd worry about her things later, when she wasn't terrified out of her mind.

Chapter 7

Jamie streaked through the upstairs, the tail of her towel flapping against the back of her calves as she sprinted softly on the balls of her feet, looking for her friend and leaving a trail of partial footprints on the dust-covered hardwood floor behind her.

"Darlene?" she whispered loudly as she passed by a closed door on her right, hoping for a response. When none came, she continued to the end of the hall, where it came to an intersection. She looked left to see four doors down a narrow hallway, two on either side wall, directly across from each other. The hallway itself seemed to come to an abrupt end beyond the second set of doors. She then looked to her right to see a similar pattern of doorways down the other passageway, but at the end, the hallway split again in two directions. She opted for the easier route so she wouldn't get lost.

Slowing her pace down the left hallway, Jamie's attention shifted to the ornate picture frames adorning the walls. Oddly, there were no pictures or portraits to admire within the frames, only large black squares made of cloth, stretched to fill the void within the wooden borders. She peered over her shoulder out of curiosity and noticed the same down the right hallway. She furrowed her brow and shook her head, wondering if the blank frames were meant to create a more eerie atmosphere for the haunted house's visitors. It was working. Sauntering forward, her stride became heavier with each slow, cautious step.

"Darlene?" she spoke again, just above a whisper. "Are you over here?" She hoped her friend was in one of the nearby rooms instead of already downstairs in the study. If not Darlene, then one of the other two women, so she wouldn't have to continue traipsing around, half-naked, looking for a safe room where she could get dressed.

She knocked on the first door to her left, to no response. She reached for the doorknob and gave it a twist, deciding, at the very least, she should put some clothes on before Chuck, or worse, Shawn, saw her in only a towel. She'd worry about finding Darlene and fixing her hair after she was decent.

Jamie slowly creaked the door open a crack to peek inside, hoping she wasn't barging in on one of the men half-dressed. Through the tiny opening, she could see that the light was off, which made her feel relieved. The house was freaky enough as it was without her having nightmares about seeing Shawn's naked, sweaty, 350 lb frame flashed at her, with the numerous rolls of skin at the base of his stomach overlapping his thighs, and the head of his shriveled penis peeking out from below his drooping belly button. The thought almost made her vomit up her morning coffee. She opened the door a little more until she felt the strands of a cobweb brush along the back of her hand, sending chills down her spine and causing her to pull away from the knob while vigorously shaking her hand to rid herself of the non-existent, man-eating tarantula that created it.

Nope, she thought while quickly grabbing the knob and slamming the door shut. *I'm not going in that room.*

The force of the door being closed caused the second door on the left to click and crack open. From her vantage point, Jamie could see just enough into the opening to notice the light escaping. Someone was there.

"Hello?" Jamie questioned. "Darlene? Are you in there? Samara?"

She slid her left hand along the wall on her way to the second door while compressing her folded clothes tighter to her chest with her right hand. With each step, she felt the air around her becoming cooler, enveloping her, until she could see her breath again with every exhale.

"Guys, who's in the room?" she asked louder, expecting someone to answer.

She placed her hand on the multi-paned, wooden door, extending her neck forward, trying to see farther into the room through the tiny opening. It was no use. If she wanted to see who, *or what*, was in the room, she'd have to open the door. Swallowing heavily, with her eyes opened wide in anxious inquisitiveness, and shivers running along her arms, her left hand softly pushed the door open, exposing more of the room, inch by inch, along its travel.

"Hello?" she said again, just as the door opened enough for her friend's back to come into view. "Oh, thank goodness, Darlene," Jamie added, her visible breath leading the way into the room.

Darlene was facing away from the door, standing beside a neatly-made, dust-covered bed, her head angled slightly downward as if she were staring at the coverings. She didn't respond to Jamie's voice, remaining silent and still.

"Darlene, what are you looking at?" Jamie asked, stepping closer to her friend and leaning sideways to try to peer around her to see what had gripped her attention. She didn't see anything but questioned again.

"Darlene?"

Nothing. Not even a slight acknowledgment.

Jamie reached forward with her left hand toward Darlene's right shoulder to gain her friend's attention.

"Darlene, are you okay?"

Just as Jamie's fingers touched the back of Darlene's shoulder, Darlene jumped and turned, startling Jamie. The cold air Jamie had felt seconds before dissipated, replaced with a warmer, stale air she'd felt before she entered the room.

"Oh, fuck!" Darlene blurted. "You scared the shit out of me."

"That makes two of us," Jamie responded. "What were you looking at?"

"What? Oh, nothing," Darlene replied, her eyes displaying a hint of fear. "It was nothing."

"Why didn't you answer me?" Jamie asked. "Didn't you hear me?"

"I must have been lost in my thoughts."

Jamie looked at her friend skeptically. "I'll say. I was right behind you, and you didn't respond."

"Yeah, uh, sorry. I-I guess I didn't hear you. Did you need something? You're not dressed. What's going on?"

"I forgot my brush at my place," Jamie replied.

"Oh, wait," Darlene said, stepping by Jamie to a backpack leaning against a dusty oak dresser. She pulled a brush out of one of the side compartments and handed it to Jamie. "Here you go."

"Thanks." Jamie tilted her head sideways like a puppy looking for acceptance and smiled. "I sorta need a place to change, too. I haven't picked out a bedroom yet. Do you mind?"

"Oh, uh, yeah. Sure."

Jamie noticed the hesitation in her friend's delivery. "I can always find another room, if you'd rather..,"

"No. Don't be silly," Darlene replied. "It's fine. Just don't forget to turn off the light when you're through."

Darlene walked to the door to exit, but stopped at the threshold. Jamie watched her friend turn sideways in the doorway to look at her, giving a nervous glare. Then, Darlene's eyes shifted to the mattress with a focused stare before meeting Jamie's eyes again.

"I'll see you downstairs," Darlene said, closing the door behind her.

Jamie blew out a breath and swiveled her head to glance at the covered mattress where her friend had been focused moments before. She scrunched her eyebrows in confusion.

What the hell was that all about?

Chapter 8

After having gotten dressed and while brushing her shoulder-length, straight brown hair, Jamie caught herself staring at the bed behind her in the mirror. She didn't know why the empty mattress intrigued her, only that it had strangely held her friend entranced, which was quite a feat since Darlene had the attention span of a flea. What was more perplexing was how Darlene brushed Jamie's inquiry aside like it was nothing. They'd always been able to tell each other anything.

Jamie gathered her things and exited Darlene's bedroom just as Pierce was stepping from the doorway directly across from her. He was holding a large butcher knife in one hand, its blade stained red, and something long in his other hand, which he quickly tucked behind his back when he saw Jamie.

"Pierce," Jamie began, her eyes wide and focused on the bloody knife, "what are you doing with that? Is that blood?"

Pierce flashed a guilt-laden smile like he'd just been caught cheating. "It's not what you think. I found it in my room. It's not even real. Touch it." He wiggled the knife quickly, and the flexible rubber blade flopped from side to side.

"I'm not touching that thing!" Jamie expressed ardently. "And I can't believe you would either."

"Why not? It's cool," he responded, slashing the knife through the air in the shape of a Z in front of his chest like he was Zorro. "It must have been a prop when this place was operating as that haunted house. What was it again? Death House?"

"Reaper House," Jamie replied. "And will you stop with the knife-playing. You're giving off creepy serial killer vibes."

Pierce frowned and dropped his arm to his side in disappointment.

"What else you got?" Jamie asked with an inquisitive grin, trying to peek around his side while he twisted away to prevent her from seeing.

"Nothing."

"Come on, Pierce; I've already seen the knife. How bad could it be?"

"Really?" he questioned. "You just called me a serial killer."

"A *creepy* serial killer," Jamie added, grinning. "Get it right. Now show me." Jamie playfully threw her hand forward, running her hand down his chest. She felt the contour of his pectoral muscle and quickly snapped her hand back, slightly embarrassed. It didn't prevent her from thinking he'd been working out since they were last together.

Pierce let out a sigh, knowing Jamie wouldn't quit until he'd given in. He always buckled under her smile. "Fine." He pulled his hand from behind his back and hesitantly swung it forward until Jamie recoiled at the sight and audibly gasped.

"Oh my God! Is that real?"

Pierce chuckled. "Of course not."

He was holding a severed appendage, the lower half of a partial right arm, cut halfway down the forearm. The cut edge was jagged and colored red, and had what appeared to be a sliver of bone protruding from the open wound. Speckled blood splashed across the realistic-looking limb down to the chipped, lavender-painted nails at the fingertips.

"I think it's silicone or something, made to look real."

"That's gross!"

Pierce followed with, "I tried to save you from seeing it."

"What are you doing with it?" Jamie asked.

"I was going to bring it down to show everyone."

"So then, I was going to see it anyway," Jamie sneered.

"Well, uh..," Pierce bit his lower lip. "I guess. But you would have been with the group, so everyone would have freaked out, not only you."

"I didn't freak out. I didn't expect something like that to be here."

"It was a haunted house, Jamie. What did you expect would be here? I bet there are all kinds of crazy things in this place."

Crazy things, Jamie thought, as her mind drifted to the electrician's odd conversation with himself, Darlene's peculiar behavior in the bedroom, and, of course, the vision of the young boy she'd seen-or thought she saw-in the bathroom.

"That's exactly why I want to get this weekend over with as quickly as possible. I could use less crazy in my life. The sooner we're out of here, the better." She nodded her head sideways. "We should get going. The others are probably waiting for us."

They began to walk toward the open landing at the top of the staircase above the foyer when Pierce nudged Jamie with his shoulder.

"So, you're staying in the room across from me, huh?"

"No, that's Darlene's room," Jamie replied. "I haven't picked a room yet."

"Oh," Pierce said excitedly. "The room next to mine is unclaimed if you want it."

Jamie could tell it was less a polite suggestion and more a hopeful request.

"Yeah, that sounds good," Jamie replied. "As long as you check it out first to make sure there's nothing scary in there."

Pierce smiled triumphantly. "I can do that."

They descended the staircase, side by side, turning right at the bottom and joining their friends in the study, the room that had been their previous night's sleeping quarters. Samara was sitting in the wing-backed chair in the center of the room, staring at Chuck while he inspected a picture on the far wall. Like the ones in the upstairs hallway, there wasn't an image, only black fabric stretched within its frame.

Vickie was sitting on one end of the lounge sofa, flipping through a Modern Style magazine, her legs curled up on the cushion beside her. Darlene occupied the other end, her eyes skyward, admiring the coffered ceiling. Shawn was standing in the front corner of the room by the window, headphones on, engrossed in his music, and casually swaying from side to side while scrolling through the song list on his phone. Jamie scanned the rest of the room, looking for the last of their party.

"Where's Brandon?" Jamie asked, anxious to begin the work for which they were all there.

Chuck responded without averting his focus from the framed picture. "He said something about checking something out somewhere."

"Thanks, Chuck," Jamie responded in a sarcastic tone. "That's very helpful."

Vickie peeked up from her magazine and spoke nonchalantly, "I saw him go outside." Then she sat up quickly, swinging her legs off the sofa and questioning enthusiastically, "Hey, what do you have there, Pierce?" directing everyone's attention his way except for Shawn, who hadn't heard a word over his music.

"I found these upstairs," he said with a huge smile, flashing his new toys. "Pretty cool, right?"

Chuck jumped in immediately, offering a jealous-sounding comment, "Big deal. They're just fake props." Then, he went back to sliding his hand along the intricate woodwork of the frame like he was caressing a woman's body.

"Were those in your room?" Vickie asked about Pierce's findings.

"Yeah." He walked to the far end of the sofa and placed the fake arm and rubber knife on the end table. "Did you guys find anything in *your* rooms?"

"Lots of dust," Vickie replied. "And an old armoire still filled with musty men's dress shirts."

"That's fun," Samara chimed in. "Chuck and I had to clear away about thirty creepy dolls from the bed."

"They weren't *all* creepy," Chuck announced.

Samara rolled her eyes. "He's only saying that because he got to fondle a naked Barbie."

Jamie shook her head at Chuck, "And I thought the *severed hand* was gross."

"What about you, Darlene?" Pierce asked. "Did you find anything interesting in your room?"

"What? Me?" she questioned with a surprised look on her face. "No. There was nothing. I didn't see anything."

Pierce squinted his eyes and smirked. "Okay, weirdo."

Then, Chuck exclaimed excitedly, "Guys, it's an opening into a little cubby."

The group looked over to witness Chuck reaching through the center of the framed black cloth.

"I couldn't even see the split line in the fabric until I ran my fingers over it."

"What's in there?" Samara asked, standing up, now curious.

"I don't know," Chuck answered. "But there's definitely something. Hold on; I've got it."

He gave a tug, and out from behind the cloth emerged an animatronic bust of a demonic-looking figure, complete with horns, sharp teeth, and dagger-like claws, posed as if it were jumping out of the wall at its intended victim. It was attached to a spring-loaded pulley that would eject the frightening demon from the picture at an appropriate moment to scare paying customers. Jamie let out a relieved breath, no longer wondering what the strange pictures on the second floor were about.

Just then, the front door slammed shut, and Brandon came running into the study, out of breath.

"Guys, there's a cemetery out back!" he shouted.

"What? Really?"

"There is?"

"No way!"

"For real?"

Even Shawn pulled his headphones from his ears. "What's going on?"

"Brandon found a cemetery out back," Chuck answered.

Only Darlene and Jamie didn't react. Jamie, because she'd already known about it and had visited it earlier that morning. Darlene, on the other hand, didn't say a word, but her face paled as if the idea of a cemetery on the property was more frightening than she'd care to admit.

"Come on, guys; we should check it out," Chuck suggested.

Jamie jumped under the study's arched entryway, blocking their path. "Whoa! Hold on. You can check out the cemetery later. We've gotta get started going through the house. We've already gotten a late start, and I do NOT want to come back here after tomorrow."

"Jamie's right, guys," Pierce added, turning to Jamie and flashing a grin. "Let's do what we need to do in the house first. We can include the cemetery viewing later as part of our party."

"Ooohh, that's a good idea," Vickie announced. "Good one, Pierce."

Jamie nodded her appreciation toward Pierce, though she'd forgotten about the party until he mentioned it. She was worried it was just one more thing to prevent them from getting the job done on time.

"Okay," Jamie began. "It's settled. Now let me explain what we need to do in here so we can leave tomorrow without any issue."

Chapter 9

Jamie distributed pads and a small box of tacks to each of her friends with instructions on what to do. They were to break up into pairs and choose a room of the house to thoroughly detail the things that needed removing, the things that needed fixing, and what needed updating. She explained to them how important it was to take their time and go though each of the rooms with a fine-toothed comb, writing down even the smallest of things, such as cracks in the drywall, discoloration on the walls above the heating vents, which could mean there are issues with the heating system, styles and finish of bathroom and kitchen fixtures, excessive gaps in the floorboards, and signs of water damage. They were to look at the windows and inspect for any cracks in the glass, black mold on the sills, and for proper sealing. She even asked that they locate and test all the outlets in the rooms by plugging something into them, preferably a working lamp, if one was handy. When they finished, they were to tack their notes outside the doorway of each room so others would know it had already been checked. This process would continue until all the rooms had been inspected. Then, Jamie would collect all the papers before they left and use them to write her final report when she got back to the office on the following Monday.

They started on the first floor, separating into their respective two-person groupings. Chuck and Samara stayed in the study, since Chuck was so enraptured by the demon erupting through the wall. Darlene and Vickie chose the kitchen. It needed some cleaning after the morning breakfast, so they volunteered to kill two birds with one stone. Shawn and Brandon opted to go through the first bedroom they found on the lower floor, which was just past the staircase on the right. Jamie paired herself with Pierce, and they began in the library.

Though she was focused on her work, it was Jamie's brief interactions with her ex that had provided her with enough distractions to forget about how scary Reaper House really was. That was comforting. Being alone with Pierce and talking with him without Chuck influencing his behavior reminded Jamie how well they jived. Their past intimacy aside, she was confident she could remain professional around him. But admittedly, the thought of trying to rekindle their relationship had crossed her mind when she decided to pair herself with him instead of Darlene. She also knew it would allow her the opportunity to question Pierce about whether he had noticed anything unusual about Darlene's behavior without causing a scene or upsetting her best friend.

"So, she didn't seem a little off to you?" Jamie asked, inspecting around the same window through which she'd earlier witnessed the electrician talking to himself.

"What do you mean by 'off'?" Pierce asked, rubbing his fingers across the built-in bookshelves along the wall beside the window. "If you ask me, she's always been a little off."

"Pierce!"

"You know what I mean," he began to explain. "I don't think Darlene ever fully recovered after..," he paused, realizing what he'd gotten himself into.

"After what?"

"Well.., after her grandmother died."

Unflinching, Jamie responded. "She was seventeen, Pierce. That was a long time ago."

He turned his head slightly and looked at her through the corner of his eye to gauge her reaction. "So, you think ten years is the time limit to get over a loved one? You know how close they were."

"That's not what I meant," Jamie replied. She thought of his words and how sincere and compassionate he sounded. The man before her was the Pierce she fell in love with.

"Tell me what *you* think then," Pierce said, stopping his progress to give his full attention to Jamie. "How has she been acting strange?"

Jamie tightened her lips and exhaled through her nose, not expecting, when she first began the conversation, to disseminate the details. But now, she felt it might help explain her concern.

"This goes nowhere, Pierce Gagnon," she said adamantly.

Pierce traced his index finger in the shape of an X across his heart.

"Earlier today, upstairs, when I first walked in on Darlene in her bedroom, she didn't hear me call out to her. I called out several times, even while I stood right behind her, but it's like she was in a daze, standing motionless, staring down at the bed. She seemed to come out of it when I touched her shoulder, but even then, she looked like she'd seen a ghost."

"A ghost?" Pierce questioned, smiling skeptically.

"Don't!" Jamie responded, pointing at him. "I know what you're thinking, and it's not like that. I'm serious. And then, in the study, when you asked if she'd seen anything interesting in her room, I specifically watched for Darlene's reaction. The way she answered - you even thought it was strange; I know you did."

"Sure, strange. But not in a 'I see dead people' sorta way. Why would you jump to that conclusion?"

Jamie bit her lower lip and felt her heart skip a beat. Bringing up her friend's odd behavior was one thing. She hadn't prepared to share her own frightening experience.

"I jumped to that conclusion because... well.., I saw something this morning."

"What?" Pierce questioned, his eyes wide. "What did you see?" He looked genuinely concerned, which Jamie appreciated.

"After my shower, I saw someone in the mirror standing behind me. I almost had a heart attack. When I turned, there was nobody there. But still, I can't get his face out of my head."

"'His?'" Pierce questioned. "It was a man?"

"It was a boy."

"A boy? Was it..?"

"No!" Jamie cut him off. "He was young, maybe a teenager. He was so white, Pierce. And his lips were purple. I swear, he looked like one of those corpses you see in the morgue before an autopsy. Like on those forensic shows. Only, he was standing right behind me, staring at me with eyes that were black as night. I couldn't stay there. I ran out of there so fast. That was how I ended up in Darlene's room.

Pierce's eyes were no longer filled with skepticism, but fear. Jamie knew he believed her. If not about there being an actual dead kid in the bath-room, at least about having seen something that scared her. He reached his arm out and pulled at her shoulder to ease her into a tender embrace against his chest. She nestled her head against him, closing her eyes and letting his muscular arms dispel all of her worries.

"It's okay, Jamie," he assured her. "I'm sure it's just this house playing tricks with your head. You don't have to worry; you're safe. I won't let anything harm you."

"Thanks, Pierce," she said, remorsefully peel-ing her head from his chest, realizing it felt dange-rously good to let it remain. She also knew they needed to get back on track with the house tasks. "Anyway, it's not a big deal. I know there's no such thing as ghosts. As for Darlene, I'm probably look-ing too much into it. She'd tell me if something was bothering her. Come on, let's get back to work."

Jamie quickly shrugged off her feelings for Pierce and began checking the outlets by plugging in an antique lamp that had been sitting on a small table beside a reading chair. Pierce strolled to the rear corner, where the built-ins took a ninety-degree turn and continued along the rear wall. He was checking the shelves for damage when he sud-denly paused, catching a glimpse of a book that caught his attention. He furrowed his brow in con-fusion.

"Didn't you say this place has been unoccupied since that old woman went crazy and killed those people?"

"Yeah, that's right," Jamie replied, carrying the lamp over to another outlet. "The town took control of the house after that, and it's been vacant ever since. Why?"

Pierce pulled a book from the shelf and studied its cover before turning it toward Jamie. "How do you suppose this book made it into the collection?"

Jamie looked up from her bent position to see what Pierce was fussing about. When she saw the book, she abandoned the lamp and rushed over to him, snatching it from his hands.

"What the hell?" she questioned. She read the cover aloud. "The tragedy of Reaper House: Halloween, Horror, and Death." She flipped the book over to glance at the rear cover. "I don't know. Someone must have come in at some point and left it here." Then, she opened the front of the book and stopped at the copyright page. Her face scrunched in puzzlement.

"What is it?" Pierce asked.

"This doesn't make any sense. The copyright date on this book is 2003. Isabelle Unger killed those people on Halloween night, 2009."

"It's gotta be a misprint," Pierce stated. "There can't be a book about true events that happened six years before they happened."

"Yeah, that's very strange. Where did you get this from?"

"Right over here." Pierce pointed to an empty slot between two books: Dark Place and Dark Lane.

Jamie looked at the vacant spot and tilted her head. "Hey, what's this?" She squeezed her open hand vertically into the available space until her fingers depressed a rocker switch at the back of the shelf. Like in a movie, one of the bookshelf panels along the rear wall clicked open.

Chapter 10

Vickie dropped the last of the silverware into the soapy water to Darlene's chagrin. Darlene rolled her eyes at her friend, who delivered the dirty dishes to her one at a time, pinching them between her thumb and index finger like she was afraid to get her hands dirty. While Darlene finished washing the dishes, Vickie began opening and closing the many cabinets in the large kitchen. If you asked her, she'd say she was checking their functionality, as well as the condition of the shelves within, but really, she was curious to see what was inside each.

"I can't believe everything was left as it was," Vickie said, opening an upper set of cabinet doors on Darlene's left. "Old dishes, furniture, and who knows what else? I mean, look at this place. You'd think somebody would have raided it by now."

"As long as they didn't leave the bodies be-hind," Darlene responded. "Besides, you just said the magic words, *'Look at this place.'* You've seen the outside. You know the house's history. I bet the kids in this backwater town wouldn't be caught dead even coming up that long-ass driveway. You'd have to be into some freaky-ass shit to want to break into *this* house."

"*We're* here, aren't we?"

"Like I said: Freaky-ass shit. I mean, come on.., Shawn, Brandon? Hell, even you and I aren't exactly what folks would call 'normal.' Besides, we didn't break in."

"Right, we volunteered to help our crazy friend," Vickie added. "Which makes us even crazier."

"Hey, Jamie's not crazy," Darlene defended her best friend. "She's just been through a lot."

"We've all been through a lot, Darlene. Even you. But none of us ever…"

"Don't say it," Darlene snapped, splashing a cup into the water and turning to face Vickie. "You know as well as I do that was a tough time in her life. She needed our support, and we turned our backs on her."

"It's not like we could have done anything," Vickie retorted. "She brought it on herself. I feel bad for Pierce after what she put him through."

"Are you kidding me right now?" Darlene erupted, gripping the knife she'd been washing tightly within her fist. "If anyone should have stood by her side, it was Pierce. He walked away. That was his choice."

"If you ask me, it wasn't much of a choice."

"Well, I didn't ask you, so shut the fuck up."

"What's your problem?" Vickie raised her voice. "You're not the only one who got hurt. We all lost a friend that day."

"Yeah. Only.., Jamie lost four friends." Darlene curled the corner of her upper lip, aggravated that they were even having the conversation.

Vickie glanced down at Darlene's clenched fist resting on the counter, her knuckles white with rage, and the blade in her trembling hand shimmering under the overhead light. Vickie's eyes widened as she took a step back.

"Maybe we should calm down and concentrate on the kitchen," she offered, shifting her eyes to meet Darlene's before letting them drift back to the knife.

Darlene noticed Vickie's nervous reaction and subtle eye movements and followed them down to her own hand, where she clutched the knife vigorously. She instantly snapped her fingers open, dropping the knife she hadn't realized she was holding onto the butcher block counter. The knife hit the wood and slid several inches from her. Vickie hesitantly reached for the knife, keeping her eyes on Darlene, picked it up, and placed it blade-side down into the dish strainer.

"Yeah, uh..," Darlene began, swallowing hard. "Right. The kitchen stuff." She pulled the drain plug to empty the sink. "Let me grab my pad and pen."

The two worked diligently, making note of the worn linoleum flooring, the chips in the countertops, the rust-colored stains in the large, white porcelain basin sink, and the dated cabinetry that spanned three of the four walls. The refrigerator and stove were a dirty mustard color, holdovers from the 1970s, that would need updating. While Vickie was jotting down the condition of the ceiling, which had faded from white to a smoky gray and had blotches of red above the stove top like there'd been an explosion of pasta sauce at some point, Darlene gravitated to the freestanding pantry cabinet. She opened the double doors and stood fixed, staring at the empty shelves.

Vickie looked around her and used the back of the pen to scratch her head.

"This place needs to be gutted. I mean, what are we even doing this for? I say, take a match and burn it to the ground."

Darlene didn't immediately respond, but a moment later, she murmured something unintelligible.

"What was that?" Vickie asked, turning toward her friend.

Without turning from the shelves, Darlene answered, "I said, *'Why are you here, Ricky?'*" Her speech was sedate, her voice raspy.

Vickie furrowed her brow and frowned. "Why would you call me that?"

"*It's your name, isn't it?*" Darlene replied in the same deliberate tone.

"That hasn't been my name in over two years. You know that."

"*I know many things. Ricky DeStello, born to Robert and Tina DeStello in the year of the forsaken son: nineteen hundred and ninety-eight. Brother, Todd. Sister, Harmony - deceased.*"

"How did you know about my sister?" Vickie asked. "She died when she was a baby. I never talk about her."

"*Death holds no secrets from me.*"

"What the hell are you talking about? And what's with your voice?"

Suddenly, Darlene's voice softened, but it was still not her own. "*What did I tell you, Ricky? You have to be careful with your sister. You can't shake her like that.*"

"Wh-what did you say?" Vickie questioned in disbelief, her eyes wide.

With yet another voice change, Darlene continued. "*But Mom, she keeps putting my Pokémon cards in her mouth.*"

"Shut up," Vickie said under her breath. "How...how do you know this?"

"Ricky, what are you doing in here?" Darlene asked in the first voice, then switching back and forth between the two.

"It...it was an accident."

"What was an accident? Oh my God! Harmony!"

"It was an accident, Mom."

"What did you do, Ricky? Oh my God! She's not breathing. Bob, call an ambulance."

"I'm sorry, Mommy."

"Get out of here, Ricky!"

"But, Mom..,"

"I said, Get out! Bob! It's Harmony. Our baby's not breathing; call an ambulance!"

Tears trickled down Vickie's cheek. "Why are you doing this? How did you even know?"

"I told you, Ricky," Darlene replied, still facing away from her friend and speaking with the methodical, raspy voice. *"Death holds no secrets from me."*

"I told you, I'm not Ricky anymore. Why are you doing this?"

"Riiiiicky."

"I said, shut up, Darlene!"

"Ricky's got a dicky."

"Shut up!"

"Licky my dicky."

"You fucking bitch," Vickie yelled, storming over to Darlene. "You don't know when to shut your fucking mouth."

Vickie grabbed Darlene's shoulder and aggressively spun her around. Upon seeing her face, Vickie jumped back.

Darlene's expression was blank, her face as pale as a sheet, but her eyes were black as coal.

"Oh shit! Oh fuck! What the..? Fuck this shit!"

Vickie immediately ran out of the kitchen in a frenzy, her heart racing. She didn't wait around long enough to witness her friend open her mouth and let out a guttural laugh.

Chapter 11

"**S**top touching that, Shawn."

Shawn ignored Brandon's words, feeling it was a better idea to continue exploring the animatronic mannequin propped in the corner of the bedroom. The mannequin, a full-size replica of a man, was dressed in light blue scrubs and was wearing a white surgical mask over its nose and mouth. The figure had one eyebrow raised, and it was easy to determine there was a sinister smile hiding beneath the mask. Both arms were extended forward, his right hand open with his fingers splayed like he was reaching to grab someone. His left hand held a scalpel.

"This thing is cool," Shawn responded, inching his head closer to the surgeon's face to check out the fine detail. "Pure artistry."

"We're supposed to be cataloging everything wrong with the room."

"Uh-huh," Shawn replied, surveying the electronic strip affixed to the mannequin's back.

"I'm serious, Shawn," Brandon urged. "Jamie's going to think we didn't do anything. Besides, you shouldn't be touching that thing. You'll get electrocuted or something."

"Don't be ridiculous, Brandon. It's not plugged in. Even if it was, it's been sixteen years since it was last in use. It probably doesn't even carry a charge."

"That's a battery, stupid. Electrical doesn't work that way."

"Whatever. You go ahead and start inspecting the room; I'll join you in a bit."

"I'll give you five minutes," Brandon said. "I'm not doing this alone."

Shawn huffed, shaking his head as he continued trying to manipulate the surgeon's articulated arms. Brandon started his task near the doorway, noting holes in the sheetrock and the exposed wiring above the light switch where the cover plate was missing. He flipped the switch off and on a few times to check its functionality. The flickering lights distracted Shawn, who swiveled his torso to look up at the overhead light fixture, causing his hand to brush against the scalpel.

"Ouch! Damn it!" Shawn cried, looking at the slice across his index finger and the blood from it, dripping to the floor.

"What?" Brandon questioned. "What happened?"

"I cut myself," Shawn said, turning to face Brandon and bringing his cut finger to his mouth to suck on the wound.

"You cut yourself?"

"On the scalpel. The goddamn thing is real."

"A real scalpel? Wouldn't that be some kind of safety violation or something?" Brandon's eyes shifted to the mannequin's, which were peering at him over Shawn's shoulder. He could have sworn he noticed one eye twitch, but didn't have time to process it as Vickie charged into the room, out of breath, and with a terrified look on her face.

"Thank God I found you guys!" she said, sounding anxious and desperate.

"What's going on, Vickie?" Brandon asked. "What's the matter?"

"It's Darlene. I don't know what the fuck happened. She was acting all crazy and shit. Her face was whiter than mine, and her eyes were rolled back in her sockets, or something. They were pitch black. Like, fucking black."

"Slow down, slow down," Brandon said, tapping his hand a couple of times on Vickie's shoulder to calm her and then resting his hands there to steady both of them. "Did you check to see if she was okay? Maybe she was having a seizure."

"It wasn't a fucking seizure, Brandon. She was saying all kinds of weird shit. I'm telling you, she wasn't herself."

"Where is she?"

"I left her ass in the kitchen and ran until I found you," Vickie said between gulping breaths.

"Well, we've got to check on her. There could be something wrong."

Shawn spoke up, "Ah, yeah.., you guys go. I think I'll stay here."

Brandon rolled his eyes. "Come on, Vickie."

"What? You expect me to go back in there?"

"Just come on; you can stay behind me."

They both exited the bedroom on their way to the kitchen with Vickie snuggled up close to Brandon, her breath on the back of his neck, sending goosebumps down his arms.

"I'm telling you," Vickie said in a whisper, "something wasn't right. That wasn't her."

"What kind of weird stuff was she saying?" Brandon asked.

Vickie felt her heart thump in her chest. She couldn't share the information. She'd held onto the guilt for so long and promised she'd never tell anyone what happened that day.

"I don't know. Just messed up stuff," Vickie stuttered. "And her voice was weird, too."

They shuffled down the hallway and broached the kitchen entryway, where they saw Darlene squatting in front of an open lower cabinet door, scribbling notes on her pad. She turned her head to them, an annoyed look on her face.

"What the fuck, Vickie? You're gonna make me do all the work myself? Are you that afraid to get your precious hands dirty?"

"What are you talking about? I was working, too, until you started saying all that creepy shit."

"Creepy shit? We were talking about how we both landed that job at Tucker's after high school, and then you told me to shut up, and you stormed out of here."

"That's not what happened."

"What are you talking about? That's exactly what happened. You told me how much fun you had there, and when I said how much I missed working for Mr. Tucker, you balled up your fists, yelled at me, and ran out."

Brandon turned to Vickie with a questioning look.

"She's lying!" Vickie stated emphatically. "That's not how it happened, and she knows it. She was acting crazy. I thought she was going to stab me at one point."

"Stab you?" Darlene questioned, scrunching her face. "What the hell?"

"That's right. With that knife over there." Vickie traipsed across the kitchen to the sink, where she dug through the dish strainer looking for the knife. "It's not here. What did you do with it?"

"Do with what? I don't know what you're talking about."

Vickie clenched her teeth and charged toward Darlene, stopping in front of her.

"You know what I'm talking about. I don't know why you're doing this. No, I take that back. I know why you're doing it. Because you're a fucking bitch."

Darlene's jaw dropped as Vickie stormed past Brandon on her way out of the kitchen.

"What the fuck was that about?" Darlene questioned rhetorically behind a flabbergasted chuckle, her eyes wide in shock.

"Did you guys have too much caffeine this morning?" Brandon asked jokingly.

Darlene shook her head in frustration. "Whatever. I can't deal with her messed-up shit. I'll get more done without her in my way."

"You good?" Brandon asked.

"I'm good."

"Okay," he responded, throwing his thumb over his shoulder. "I guess I'm gonna get back to it then."

"You do that."

Brandon exited the kitchen and sauntered back down the hall toward the bedroom. When he stepped into the doorway, he wasn't at all surprised to see Shawn still fidgeting with the animatronic surgeon. Shawn heard him enter and turned to face him.

"Is everything worked out between those two?"

"Hardly. I don't think they like each other very much."

"That's why I don't involve myself in women's matters," Shawn said with a corny smile on his face.

Just then, Brandon's eyes shot open in horror as the mannequin behind Shawn came alive, raising its scalpeled hand high over Shawn's head. Panicked, Brandon yelled, "Shit! Run! It's alive." He ran from the room, not looking back at the horror that was about to befall his friend.

Chapter 12

Samara didn't know what it was that attracted her to Chuck. They'd known each other since grade school, but never once did she think of him as relationship-worthy. He had the looks, with his infectious smile and curly blonde hair that was reminiscent of Heath Ledger in A Knight's Tale, but he lacked the personality she was looking for in a boyfriend. He was never serious enough.

She always assumed she ended up with Chuck out of convenience. Maybe it was that she'd been single for too long after her previous four-year relationship ended that she missed the companionship. The togetherness. Maybe she was sexually frustrated and wanted to feel the touch of a man's hands on her skin again. Or maybe it had more to do with his insistent pestering. Whatever her reason, Chuck was available for her needs, and she jumped in headfirst, throwing caution to the wind.

Surprisingly, in the six months they'd been dating, she hadn't regretted her decision, even when he joked about serious matters.

"I'm telling you, Samara, I'm pretty sure this is the chair where the old lady killed herself."

"I don't think so," Samara answered. "I'm sure the police would have confiscated it."

"No, I'm telling you; I can see blood stains in the fabric."

"That's gross, then, because you slept on it last night."

"You sat in it earlier."

"That's how I know it's not the same chair; I would never sit in a chair that somebody died in."

"You realize that doesn't make any sense."

"It makes sense to me, and that's all that matters."

Samara grabbed a dusty, brass lamp from the table at the far end of the sofa. It looked like a tall, thin candlestick holder with a tan hexagonal lamp shade that had gemstone tassels dangling from the bottom edge. She strode to the rear wall behind the wing-backed chair and squatted near an outlet below a shelf with a stuffed fisher on it. Chuck was along the front wall, playing with the locks on the windows. Samara plugged in the lamp and clicked it to the on position with the twist-knob. The bulb lit up, to her surprise.

"I can't believe this bulb still works after all these years," she said more to herself than to

Chuck. When she clicked the light off, she heard Chuck mumble something to her.

"What did you say?" she asked, shuffling to the next outlet on her left.

"I didn't say anything."

"Oh." She plugged the lamp into the next outlet and watched the lamp glow, though she hadn't turned the knob yet. Then she heard Chuck again.

She responded, "What, babe?"

"What, what?" he replied.

"What did you say?"

"I told you, I didn't say anything."

Samara stood and turned in his direction, annoyed, the lamp still in her hand. She could see the top of his blonde curls sticking up over the top of the wing-backed chair.

"I heard you say something, Chuck. Stop fooling around. And you're supposed to be working, not sitting."

Upon hearing that, Chuck stood up from where he was kneeling beneath the windows and replied, "What are you talking about, hon? I *am* working."

Her eyes lifted to see him across the room, then darted back to the chair to figure out what it was she'd seen, but it was empty.

"How did you..?"

"What?" he questioned.

Just then, the bulb from the lamp Samara was holding exploded, spraying glass in all directions. She threw the lamp in shock and jumped back.

Chuck rushed to her. "Whoa! Are you all right?"

"Yeah, I'm fine. I mean, I'll be fine once my heart starts again. Shit!"

While Samara caught her breath, they heard stomping in the hall coming toward them. They both turned to see what the commotion was and watched Vickie race past the study doorway and clamber up the staircase.

"What's that all about?" Chuck asked.

"I don't know; something's upset her."

"When *isn't* she upset about something?"

"Chuck! Be nice."

"I'm just saying; you know how she gets."

Then, they heard a second commotion out in the hall and turned again to witness Brandon running frantically for the front door. They heard the door open, followed by a loud slam.

"What the hell is going on around here?" Chuck questioned, racing for the hallway with Samara right behind him.

They opened the front door to question Brandon about what was wrong, but when they looked out, he was already on his motorized scooter, heading down the long driveway. They yelled to him, but it was of no use. He was already too far away to hear them, and he probably wouldn't have turned back if he had.

"What was that about?" Chuck questioned.

"I have no idea." Samara had a look of concern on her face.

"Well, something's going on," Chuck said, closing the door. "You go up and check on Vickie; I'll find Shawn."

Chapter 13

Back in the library, Jamie squeezed the strange book they'd found tightly in her hand as she and Pierce pulled the hinged bookshelf open to reveal a stone staircase leading down into complete darkness. Jamie looked at Pierce with fright in her eyes and shook her head.

"I'm not going down there," she offered.

"You expect me to go down there alone?"

"No. I don't think either of us should go. We don't know what's down there."

"It's a basement," Pierce responded. "Furnace, water heater..."

"Dead bodies," Jamie interrupted.

"Stop. You're only scaring yourself more; this isn't the movies."

"It's a secret door cut into a bookshelf leading down to a creepy-looking dungeon inside a haunted house where twelve people were murdered. I'm pretty sure scary is what they were going for. Can't we just close the door and pretend we never found it?"

"That wouldn't be right," Pierce said. "There could be something down there that your boss will need to know about. There could be flooding, mold, asbestos, or even a crumbling foundation." He fumbled his hand along the walls inside the doorway until he found what he was looking for. "Ah-ha! We have light." He flipped a switch, and the stairway illuminated from a light source below to show five stone ledges of slate leading down to a larger stone landing, where the stairs then took a sharp left turn, descending out of sight. "What do you say? Ready to find some hidden treasures?"

Jamie bit her lower lip, struggling with a decision. She realized Pierce was trying to lighten the situation to keep her calm, but he hadn't been through what she'd been through.

"You know I'm not good with this stuff."

"I know. But you're stronger now. And I'll be with you; I won't let you down this time." Pierce offered her a comforting smile.

"Stay close," she said with worried eyes.

"You know I will. I'll go first, and you can hold onto the back of my shirt."

Jamie swallowed heavily, took in a deep breath, let it out, then nodded.

"Okay, here we go," Pierce affirmed with a waning confidence he wouldn't allow himself to show, as he stepped down onto the first slate step. Jamie gripped the lower hem of his t-shirt with her empty hand and followed his lead. She instinctively reached behind her with her other hand, wishing there was someone to grab onto. When she realized what she'd done, she pulled it back and rested it, along with the book, on Pierce's shoulder blade.

They descended the hard steps. Pierce brushed away the cobwebs in his path until they reached the first landing. He peeked to his left to get an idea of what they were getting themselves into. There were another five steps leading down to a concrete floor, where overhead lights revealed an open space in Pierce's immediate line of sight. He saw rows of stacked cardboard boxes, three high, piled along one wall.

"What do you see?" Jamie asked, tucking her head into the back of Pierce's shoulder.

"It looks like an ordinary basement. There are boxes."

Jamie shifted her head up to peek over his shoulder.

"See? Nothing to worry about," Pierce assured her. "Let's check it out."

Jamie continued to cling to Pierce's shirt as they eased their way down the last of the steps to the basement floor. She surveyed the surroundings to calm her nerves. Along the wall at the base of the steps were the boxes Pierce had mentioned. On the opposite wall were the furnace and water heater Pierce had correctly guessed, along with a large, corroded steel basin sink. The third wall at the far end of the basement contained more of the frames with black cloth - dozens of them - overlapping and leaning against the wall. And finally, along the wall behind the stairs, the only place where the light didn't reach, only darkness.

"It's dry," Pierce noted. "That's a good sign."

"Great. Can we get out of here now?"

"Hold on; don't you want to see what's in the boxes?" Pierce asked, stepping to the nearest stack and pulling the top box down to the floor.

"Not particularly."

Ignoring Jamie's plea, Pierce opened the top flaps of the box.

"Hey, check this out," he said, grabbing Jamie's attention. "It's full of plastic weapons. Knives, hatchets, arrows, sickles, small bats, there's even a lug wrench in here." He picked up a knife and twirled it in his fingers.

"Got it. Let's go," Jamie urged.

"Wait; one more." He grabbed the second box and placed it beside the first.

"Okay, but last one, then let's get out of here."

While Pierce fumbled with removing the tape from the box, Jamie looked around her nervously, biting the skin at the side of her fingernails. Her heart was beating through her ribs while her other hand gripped the book tightly to her chest. Then, from behind her back, she heard scuffling. Her eyes darted to the darkness beyond the stairs. She squinted, trying to get her eyes to adjust to the black shroud as she felt for her phone in her back pocket. The air around her suddenly became thin and frigid. Goosebumps shot up her arms, landing at the base of her neck, where they crawled down her spine, causing her to shiver. She pulled her phone out and held it at arm's length, shining the flashlight into the dark space, but the unforgiving blackness swallowed it up without giving away its secrets.

"Pierce, I think we should go," Jamie said, watching her breath exit her mouth.

"Yeah, in a sec," he replied, his attention fixed on the box.

Another scuffling sound came from the darkness, closer this time, like someone's shoe scraping along the concrete.

"Pierce, I mean it. I think someone's down here. We need to go."

Pierce turned his head to look at Jamie over his shoulder. "What are you talking about?"

Just then, loud thunderous sounds came from overhead, raining dust and debris on them from between the floorboards in the ceiling above. Jamie didn't pay heed, keeping her widened eyes glued on the disappearing light of her phone. Pierce looked up in curiosity.

"What the hell is going on up there?"

Jamie didn't respond; her stare held firm where she'd heard the scraping noises.

Pierce stood, dusting himself off. "We should find out what all the commotion is about."

Jamie tilted her head sideways and took a step toward the wall of darkness. Whispers called her forward.

"Jamie," the whisper summoned. *"You've arrived."*

Pierce stepped onto the bottom slab of rock to head back up, then stopped when he realized Jamie hadn't reacted to his suggestion.

"Jamie?" he questioned, seeing her mesmerized gaze. "What are you looking at?"

Jamie didn't acknowledge him, taking another step closer to where the darkness engulfed the light.

"Come to us, Jamie," the whispers continued. *"Leave it behind. Follow my voice."*

"Jamie!" Pierce said louder.

Nothing. No response except another step forward.

"Jamie. We've been waiting for you. Don't you want to join us? Come to us, Jamie. Come to us now."

"Jamie."

"Jamie."

"Jamie!" Pierce yelled, grabbing her by the shoulder and spinning her around.

She looked dazed and somewhat confused, but focused on his words.

"What's wrong with you?" Pierce asked. "Didn't you hear me?"

"What? No. I mean.., yes. I hear you."

"Then let's go. Something's going on upstairs."

She nodded, her thoughts in a fog. As they ascended the first flight of stone steps, she took a final, uneasy glance into the enveloping blackness.

Chapter 14

Pierce shoved the open bookshelf back in place while Jamie rushed to the arched threshold at the library's entrance. There, she saw Samara at the top of the main staircase, and Chuck swerving around the newel post at the bottom on his way down the long hallway. She called to him.

"Chuck!"

He grabbed one of the balusters to stop his forward momentum and turned to her.

"We heard running," she said. "What's going on?"

"That's what we're trying to find out," he replied, just as Pierce appeared over Jamie's shoulder. "Vickie ran upstairs looking upset, and Brandon charged out of here like the place was on fire. He took off on his scooter. Samara went upstairs to check on Vickie. I was going to find Shawn."

"What about Darlene?" Jamie asked.

"What *about* me?" Darlene spoke up from behind Chuck, causing him to jump.

"Oh shit!" he cried, bending over and grabbing his chest. "Don't do that."

"*You're* going to act like a damn sissy, too?" Darlene questioned.

"I'm not a sissy. I didn't hear you sneak up on me, is all."

"Enough, you too," Jamie jumped in. "Jesus, it's like I'm watching over a bunch of kindergarteners. Darlene," she nudged her chin up the stairs, "what happened with Vickie?"

"Damned if I know," Darlene replied. "One minute we were talking, then the next she was acting like a psycho and stormed off."

"What were you two talking about that would have made her so upset?"

"Nothing."

"Nothing?"

"We were talking about our old job, and then suddenly, bam, she got pissed off and ran out. I told you she was going to be a problem. She's so dramatic. If you ask me, it's all just an act so she doesn't have to get her hands dirty."

Then a voice came from behind Darlene.

"Hey, guys."

That time, both Darlene and Chuck jumped as one. Shawn stood oblivious, smiling while raising his hand in a sort of wave.

"Christ, Shawn!" Darlene blurted. "What the fuck?"

"Who's the sissy now?" Chuck asked with a smirk on his face.

"Shut up," she retorted.

"Shawn," Jamie began, "Brandon was with you, wasn't he?"

"Yeah."

"Why did he go running out of here?"

"I think he was afraid of the surgeon."

"The...what?"

"Oh yeah, the surgeon," he answered, pointing behind him to the bedroom. "It's another animatronic dummy like the demon thing in the study. I found the remote and activated it."

"The batteries still worked?" Chuck questioned.

"That's just it," Shawn replied, "I checked. There were no batteries *in* it. I can't figure out how the damn thing moved. But it did, and I think Brandon thought the thing came to life, or something. As soon as he saw it move, he ran out of the room with his tail tucked between his legs."

"Well, that's just great," Jamie said, annoyed. "You made him leave. Chuck said he took off on his scooter."

"Are you serious?" Darlene questioned. "He hightailed it out of here because of a dummy?"

"Well, it is an *animatronic* dummy," Shawn spoke up.

"I was talking about *you*, dumbass," Darlene responded.

"Oh."

"Can someone please call Brandon and get him back here?" Jamie asked.

Pierce, Chuck, and Shawn pulled out their phones like it was a race to see who could be the hero. They all tapped their phones and made grumbling noises.

"Does anyone have service?" Pierce asked.

"I've got nothing," Shawn answered.

"No bars for me," Chuck added.

"What about in the study?" Jamie questioned. "Remember last night, Brandon said something about his phone not working in the hallway."

Chuck backed up into the study, staring at his screen. "Nope. I still.., no wait. I've got one bar."

Just then, the front door burst open, scaring all present in the foyer. Standing in the doorway with a panicked look was Brandon.

"Oh, good, you came back," Jamie said, catching her breath after being startled.

"I didn't have a choice," Brandon replied. "There's a tree across the driveway.

"A tree?" Pierce questioned.

"Yeah. I would have gone around, but it's overhanging where the land drops off on either side."

"How big is it? Can we move it?"

"Nobody's moving that thing without a bull-dozer," Brandon answered.

"Shit! How are we going to get out of here?"

"I'm going to have to call someone," Jamie said. "The fire department, maybe?"

Chuck jumped in, "You do that, Jamie. The rest of us guys will go check it out, see if we can budge it at all."

"Me too?" Shawn questioned.

"*Especially* you, Shawn," Chuck replied. "You're the biggest of us."

Brandon's face lit up. "Shawn! You're alive!"

"Yeah. I was trying to show you I found the remote for the surgeon, but you took off."

"You big jerk," Brandon responded, a smile on his face.

"Okay, you girls stay here in case the other two come downstairs," Pierce said. "They'd probably freak out if we were suddenly all gone. We'll go and figure out the tree situation."

The guys started out the door, led by Brandon. Chuck and Shawn were next, followed by Pierce. Before he closed the door, Jamie called to him.

"Pierce."

He looked at her from around the door.

"Be careful."

He winked. "I'm always careful."

Chapter 15

J amie stared at her phone, shaking her head in frustration, watching the single bar of cell service flicker on and off. She slowly strolled around the study, raising and lowering her phone, hoping for something more consistent so she wouldn't have to use the emergency call button. It was no use.

"I'm not getting any service," she said to her friend while continuing to stare at her screen. "How about you?"

Darlene scowled, "I've got nothing. Maybe it's the walls. We might have better luck outside."

"I'll go out," Jamie offered. "Why don't you check on Vickie and Samara?"

"I don't know if that's such a good idea. It might be better if you go upstairs instead. I'll go out and check for service. I think Vickie is upset with me for some reason. There's no need to add to her tantrum."

Jamie flashed a concerned look.

"What?" Darlene questioned, shrugging her shoulders. "I didn't do anything. I swear."

Jamie exhaled from her nose. "Fine. I'll go up. If you get anything, look up tree services. Maybe someone can come out here before it gets too late."

"Okay," Darlene agreed, heading for the exit, "but I think it's going to come down to the locals coming here with chainsaws and axes."

Darlene stepped out of the front door onto the porch while Jamie marched up the staircase, two steps at a time. When she got to the second floor, she realized she had no idea where Vickie's room was. By process of elimination, she knew it wasn't down the left hallway. She hoped they'd left the door open to make it easy for her, but if not, and if Vickie was as heated as everyone made it sound, Jamie was sure to hear her complaining.

She ventured right and noticed immediately that all the doors were closed.

"Of course," she mumbled under her breath. "Vickie?" she announced loudly. "Samara? Are you guys over here?" She listened for a response. There was only silence. "Vickie?" she questioned again, stopping at the first set of doors and knocking on the one to her right. "It's Jamie. Are you in there?" She began to reach for the knob but remembered the cobwebs that had clung to her hand from the previous attempt down the other hallway and thought better of it. She glanced at the door across from her, listened intently, then shook her head. She continued forward, walking ever so softly like she was walking on eggshells, listening for any signs of life. "Guys? Are you down here?"

Favoring the wall on her right, she reached the second set of doors and was about to knock when she heard giggling from within. *There you are*, she thought, relief washing over her as she grabbed the knob. "I was beginning to think," she began, as she swung the door open, "that I was going..."

She froze, looking into an empty bedroom, where the wall ahead of her carried the stained remnants of blood spatter arching upward toward the ceiling. Jamie's blood ran cold as she took in a shallow breath, her eyes locked on the terrifying sight like a car wreck you can't look away from. Suddenly, she felt a chill, as the hair along her arms stood erect from the cold and the terror. She slowly backed out, pulling the door closed.

"Oh my God," she whispered, closing her eyes and leaning her head against the doorframe. While trying to catch her breath, she heard a creaking sound behind her. Her eyes sprang open, and she slowly, cautiously turned to her left, her heart beating like a drum. She saw that the door along the opposite wall was cracked open about two inches, but looked dark inside.

"Samara, Vickie, are you in there?" Jamie stepped forward, reaching for the knob of the open door. Just before she grasped it in her hand, the door slammed shut, causing her to jump and pull her hand away like she'd touched a hot burner.

"Shit!" she blurted just before a hand grabbed her right shoulder from behind.

"Aaagghhh!" she screamed, spinning around in defensive mode and slamming her back against the door that had just closed. Standing in front of her with aghast looks on their faces were Vickie and Samara. Vickie was still tightly gripping the knob of the door they'd just exited. More so because of Jamie's scream. "Jesus Christ!" Jamie let out, grabbing her chest. "You scared the shit out of me."

"Sorry," Samara responded. "We thought you heard us come out."

"Well, I didn't," Jamie said, bending over and grabbing her knees for stability. "Why didn't you guys answer me?"

"We heard you call for us," Vickie answered. "That's why we came out."

"Wait; from that room?" Jamie questioned, nodding her head toward the door Vickie was standing in front of.

"Um, yeah," Vickie replied, furrowing her brow confusedly, wondering where else Jamie thought they would have come from.

"I just looked. You weren't in there."

Samara turned and looked at Vickie, and then back at Jamie with a puzzled gaze. "Yeah, we were."

"No, you weren't. Not unless you were hiding from me to be funny."

"Jamie," Vickie jumped in, "we were sitting on the bed the whole time. You never came in."

"I did. There wasn't anything in there except blood all over the wall?"

"Blood? On the Wall?" Samara asked. "What are you talking about?"

"The blood," Jamie repeated, louder. "It was splattered all over the wall." She slipped by Samara and brutishly nudged Vickie to the side so she could open the door. "How could you guys not have noticed it?" she continued, as she swung the door open to show them.

Jamie felt her stomach twist in a knot as she peered across the room at the unstained wall, the light pink floral pattern on the wallpaper mocking her.

"No, that's not right," Jamie argued softly to herself. "I was just in here. There was dark-colored, dried blood splattered all over that wall."

"Are you all right, Jamie?" Samara asked.

Jamie shook her head, confused. "I...I could have sworn..."

Vickie looked at Samara behind Jamie's back and rolled her eyes. Samara squinted and subtly shook her head.

Vickie exhaled heavily, "Well, this has been fun, girls," she said sarcastically. "Thanks for the pep talk. I think I'll go hang myself from the chandelier now."

"What?" Jamie said sternly, her mind jumping to the thought of Rory Wilkinson, dangling from the fixture. "Why would you say something like that?"

"Relax; it was a joke," Vickie said. "There's no way I'm going to let myself die in a place like this."

She shook her head playfully and walked away in the direction of the staircase. Jamie had a sour look plastered on her face as she watched Vickie turn the corner. She turned her head to her left to look back into the room she'd sworn had blood on the wall, and stared blankly, dumbfounded.

"Are you sure you're okay?" Samara questioned again.

Jamie nodded, though her mind was screaming, *No, I'm not okay*.

"I'm gonna go back downstairs then," Samara said, throwing her thumb over her shoulder. "Are you coming?"

Suppressing her thoughts, Jamie faked a grin, "Yeah. Yeah, I'm coming. Let's go." She closed the door and scrambled down the hall to join Samara. After what she'd seen – what she *thought* she saw – she couldn't get away from that area fast enough.

Chapter 16

Chuck scratched the back of his head as he stood in awe at the size of the massive oak tree sprawled across the dirt driveway.

"Well, you weren't wrong; it's definitely blocking our way out of here."

"I told you we weren't going to be able to move it," Brandon reminded everyone.

"Shit, Brandon," Chuck began, subconsciously flexing his arm, "you obviously underestimate our strength. If we work together, we should be able to push one end of it out of the way."

"Are you out of your mind?" Pierce said, holding back a chuckle. "The thing is two feet in diameter and must be at least..," he looked toward the base end of the tree and then toward the tree top, "...seventy-five feet long."

"There are four of us, Pierce," Chuck said, fully confident in his belief. "Plus, we have Shawn. Once we get it moving a little bit, the rest will be easy."

"You're crazy, you know that?" Pierce responded.

Chuck flashed him a smile and raised and lowered his eyebrows a few times. "I know; it's why Samara loves me."

Pierce rolled his eyes and noticed a similar reaction from Shawn.

"Listen, guys," Chuck added, "we won't know unless we try. Humor me, huh."

Pierce shook his head and let out an exasperated breath from his nose. "Fine. We'll try your dumb idea, if only to prove you wrong. Let's do this," he continued, bending over and placing his hands on the rough bark.

Brandon was the first to react, jumping to Pierce's left with his hands firmly planted on the tree. He gave Pierce a nod. Pierce pursed his lips and creased his brow, then turned his head forward. Shawn was next, who shrugged his shoulders and positioned himself next to Brandon. The three of them stood pressed against the tree for a few seconds before Pierce looked up at Chuck's smug face and asked, "Are you coming?"

Chuck crossed his arms about his chest and smirked. "Are you kidding me? It's an oak tree. It's two feet in diameter and about seventy-five feet long. We're not moving that thing."

Pierce shoved himself to an upright position. "You're an idiot."

"I can't believe you guys were actually going to try to move a tree out of the way."

Shawn swiveled his head to his left to talk over his shoulder. "So, we're not going to try?"

Brandon stood and brushed his hands off. "No, Shawn. Chuck was joking and being an asshole."

"Then, somebody's gotta help me up. I'm a little too top-heavy for this shit."

Pierce and Brandon each grabbed an arm and heaved the big man to his feet.

"You guys are so gullible," Chuck said with a huge smile, pleased with himself.

"Yeah, and you're a dipshit," Pierce answered. He looked over the tree at the lonely road in the distance, at the bottom of the winding downhill driveway. "You could have lifted your scooter over the tree and kept going, Brandon. Why didn't you?"

"Well, um," he paused, looking at the other three, "I couldn't leave you guys stuck here."

"You could have gone to the police station, moron," Chuck jumped in.

"Oh. I didn't think of that. Should I go now?"

"Let's find out if Jamie already contacted the fire department or somebody else first," Pierce said, turning back to the mansion. "They're probably already on their way."

The four trekked up the driveway until they came to the bend where, in the distance, in front of Reaper House, they saw Darlene with her head slumped to her chest, trudging aimlessly in a circle. Her arms were flopped to her sides, and she seemed to be dragging her feet, kicking up dust around her.

"What is Darlene doing?" Chuck asked.

"I don't know," Pierce replied. "Come on."

They hustled the rest of the way up the driveway to their friend. As they approached, Pierce noticed Darlene's cell phone on the ground behind her, just outside the circumference of the trough her feet had dug. The noticeably shattered screen was so bad that some of the internal electronics were exposed.

"Darlene, what are you doing?" Chuck questioned.

She didn't respond, keeping her blank stare to the ground as she continued her circular path.

Pierce stepped forward and grabbed her arm. Her skin was unusually cool to the touch. "Darlene, stop!"

Upon his command, Darlene immediately stopped and looked at Pierce, confused.

"What?" she asked.

"What are you doing?"

"I'm trying to get a signal on my phone."

Pierce let go of her arm and marched to her phone on the ground, picking it up.

"Your phone is over here," he said, holding it up for her. "Broken."

Darlene scrunched her face and shook her head. "Well, I mean, I was trying to get a signal, but I must have dropped it."

"Dropped it?" Chuck responded. "It looks like you ran it over a few times."

"Yeah, shit!" she replied, grabbing it away from Pierce. "My phone."

"Do you know if Jamie got through to anyone?" Pierce asked.

"I don't know; I've been out here."

"Let's go."

Pierce nodded sideways toward the front door as he shuffled for the porch to find out.

They entered the front door to the sound of arguing coming from the study on their left. Pierce stepped into the room's arched entryway to find Jamie rubbing her forehead intensely while standing in front of Vickie, who was back to lounging on the sofa with a magazine in her hand.

"What's going on?" Pierce asked.

Samara stepped forward, "Jamie's having a hard time right now."

"Why? What's the matter?"

Vickie looked up from her reading, "Duh, it's this house. It's got her all messed up."

"I'm not messed up!" Jamie exclaimed. "There's just too much going on. I shouldn't have had you guys come up here with me."

"Hey, hey," Pierce said, stepping forward and placing his hand tenderly on her shoulder. "We volunteered."

"It doesn't matter," Jamie replied. "The place is creepy as shit, nothing's getting done, and now there's a tree blocking our way, so we can't leave."

"You couldn't get a hold of the fire department?"

"No. My phone's not working at all now." Jamie looked around Pierce's shoulder at Darlene with a questioning look. In response, Darlene waved her smashed phone in the air.

"Is anyone else's phone working?" Pierce questioned loudly.

Everyone pulled their phones out and stared at the screens. Fingers pressed frantically on the glass and the buttons, only to elicit the same response from all. Their phones were dead.

"I don't understand," Chuck said. "There's no way all of our phones can be dead. I know I had at least eighty percent battery life."

"I'm telling you," Jamie spoke up, "it's this house. And now we're all stranded here without a way to contact anyone."

"Okay," Pierce said, trying to calm Jamie down. "It's no big deal. I'm going to help Brandon lift his scooter over the tree, and he's going to ride into town and get the police or the fire department. Somebody."

"I am?"

Pierce shot him a side-eyed glare.

"I mean, I *am*."

"See?" Pierce acknowledged, smiling at Jamie to ease her anxiety. "Everything is going to be fine."

Jamie looked up at him with a nervous stare and nodded.

He patted her on the shoulder and turned to Brandon. "Okay, let's get you on your way."

Chapter 17

The silence was deafening in the study as the late afternoon sun's departure behind the treeline cast stretching shadows through the front windows, cascading across the room, and over the long faces within. Jamie sat on one end of the sofa, across from Vickie, biting her nails and staring at the book about Reaper House beside the prop arm and knife on the end table. Chuck and Samara sat on the floor in front of the unlit fireplace, cuddled close to each other, while Samara rubbed her hand up and down Chuck's pant leg. Darlene stood in front of the window, peering out at the circle she'd dug during her unresponsive march. Pierce leaned his shoulder into the wall by the arched doorway, his arms crossed, his eyes focused on Jamie. Shawn sat quietly in the wingbacked chair, shifting his stare between all

113

present, waiting for someone to speak up. Then, the moment came.

"Sitting here isn't doing us any good," Pierce said.

Jamie's eyes shifted from the book to meet his. "I don't want to be here anymore," she said. "I'll tell my boss this was a mistake, and that he'll have to check out the property himself."

"That's fine," Pierce said, "but we can't just sit here being mopey."

"Well, I don't want to go through the rooms anymore," Jamie replied.

"I agree," Vickie said, looking up from her magazine. "This place is creepy as fuck." Then she swiveled her head to look at the back of Darlene. "And the company isn't that great."

Samara's mouth gaped open at the comment, but Darlene remained motionless.

"Vickie, that's enough," Pierce said. "Listen, guys, Brandon is on his way into town. He'll get the fire department up here to get the tree taken care of, and then, we can get out of here."

"If he doesn't get lost," Chuck joked.

Pierce gave him a sour look.

"Well, I don't know about the rest of you," Vickie began, placing her magazine on the sofa cushion between her and Jamie, "but I could use a drink."

Chuck's head shot up, "Now that's the best idea I've heard all day. Let's get this party started."

"We're not having a party," Jamie stated emphatically. "Not with the fire department and possibly the police on their way."

"Jamie's right," Pierce agreed. "No party. Besides, we'll be leaving soon enough."

"I'm still having a drink," Chuck said as he got up from the floor to follow Vickie into the kitchen. "Anyone else?"

Samara quickly raised her hand, followed by Shawn. Pierce looked at Jamie, who shook her head no.

"I'll pass," Pierce said.

"What about you, Darlene?" Chuck called to her from the arched entrance. "Can I get you a drink?"

Darlene didn't move from her position. Chuck flopped his hand over in frustration as he turned to exit. "Suit yourself."

Pierce watched as Samara got up to check on Darlene. He turned back to Jamie as if to question Darlene's behavior. She shook her head and shrugged her shoulders. He went over and sat beside her.

"You doing okay?"

"I have a headache," she answered.

"Why don't you go upstairs and take a nap? It's going to be a few hours before they get the tree cleared out."

"I'm not going up there alone."

Just then, Chuck's voice erupted from around the corner.

"Drinks are served."

He and Vickie entered carrying small round trays holding several 12-oz cans of beer and filled shot glasses.

"We brought extra in case anyone changed their mind. If not.., more for me."

They placed the trays on the coffee table in front of the sofa. Samara tried to convince Darlene to have a drink, but Darlene shook her head, declining and continuing to stare out the window. Chuck picked up a can and extended it to Pierce.

"No thanks. Jamie's got a headache. I'm going to go upstairs with her so we can take a nap."

"*'Take a nap,'* huh?" Vickie said with a devilish grin as she downed a shot. "Sounds tantalizing."

"Real mature," Pierce said, standing and helping Jamie to her feet. He looked down at the tray of alcohol and back up at Chuck. "Try not to get wasted."

"Sure thing," Chuck replied, as he and Samara clanked shot glasses together before swallowing the drinks down.

"Come on," Pierce said to Jamie, allowing her to go first. They stepped from the study and made their way up the staircase. Pierce palmed her shoulders as she led the way.

"Have fun!" Chuck called out, unable to contain his giggling.

Pierce's voice echoed back from the top of the stairs, "You're still an asshole."

He escorted Jamie down the left hallway to her room.

"You didn't have to come, you know," Jamie said softly.

"Of course I did," Pierce replied. "I told you I would make sure your room was safe, didn't I?"

Jamie smiled, looking down as she nervously picked at her fingernails. "You did."

"Okay then," he said, reaching for the knob. "Shall we?"

He opened the squeaky door and peeked inside. Darkness held the room's secrets. He flipped the light switch just inside the door, relieved that the room lit up. It was a quaint little room with a neatly made queen bed against the right wall, a painted white dresser along the left with its paint peeling, a small closet door beside the dresser, and double windows along the far wall overlooking the makeshift cemetery out back. Light blue striped wallpaper covered the walls, except where some strips had worn near the ceiling and were peeling away.

"Looks safe to me," Pierce said, opening the door wider so Jamie could see. "You shouldn't have any problems getting comfortable. If you can look past all the dust in here, that is."

"Thanks, Pierce," Jamie said, stepping inside.

"Let me grab my blanket for you; you don't want to be sleeping under those things." He pointed to the musty blankets on the bed. Jamie nodded in agreement, scrunching her nose. Pierce walked out, and less than a minute later, came back and handed the blanket to her. "I'll be right next door if you need anything," Pierce said, flinching his head sideways.

"Actually..," Jamie paused, grabbing his wrist before letting her hand slide down to his hand. "Can you stay with me? Just until I nod off?"

Pierce smiled. "I can do that."

He stepped inside and closed the door behind him.

Downstairs, Vickie sat on the sofa where Jamie had vacated and grabbed the Reaper House book from the end table. "This looks interesting. Who wants to hear about how that old Unger bitch killed those people?"

Darlene reacted to those words, twisting her head over her shoulder and glaring at Vickie with wide eyes.

Shawn sat up in his chair. "I'm interested."

"Sure," Samara said, sitting back on the floor in front of the coffee table and tugging at Chuck's arm to join her. Chuck obeyed the silent command while Vickie flipped through the opening pages.

"Let's see," she began. "Where should we start?"

Chapter 18

*I*sabelle offered a kind smile to the latest group of thirteen as they exited through the rear door of the mansion onto the hazy cemetery grounds. On clearer nights, she would set the eerie mood by turning on a fog generator that she and her late husband had purchased from a small production company that was going out of business. But that night, the natural fog was especially thick, rolling in from the open field beyond, so the generator remained silent and untouched.

The guest's final stroll through the ominous-looking cemetery was always a chilling ending to the unforgettable, spooky tour. It was one in which Isabelle never traveled herself once night fell.

When the door latched shut, Isabelle's smile faded. It had been a long night, and she still had two more tours to give before closing the doors *for the season. Each of the past five years, she'd forgotten how difficult it had been without her husband to share the arduous burden of constantly trekking through the house, up and down the flights of stairs, night after night, without a reasonably-sized break between tours. The sixth year was no exception, except that she was a year older, and her legs weren't as strong as they used to be. For that reason, she rushed the previous tour, skipping the open attic space and the secret passageway to the "Hall of Tortured Souls," so that she could give herself a moment's reprieve before having to start again.*

Tired and short of breath, she made her way to the study to collapse in her favorite chair and give her aching feet a rest. She had eight minutes to relax before the next tour was to begin. She was confident it would be enough to get her through the final two tours. She closed her eyes and rubbed her palms along the cloth-covered arms of the wingback chair...

"Wait!" Chuck interrupted. "So this *is* the wingback chair the old lady sat in." He pointed to the chair currently occupied by Shawn.

"Well, it was *all* her furniture," Vickie answered snidely, "so of course she would have sat in it."

"I mean, it's the same one she killed herself in," Chuck said, winking at Samara.

"I don't know. I haven't gotten that far yet."

"Then, what are you waiting for?" Chuck questioned, opening another beer. "Keep going."

Vickie flashed him an annoyed glare, then continued.

She rubbed her palms along the cloth-covered arms of the wingback chair and tilted her head back, resting it on the rear cushioning. Her eyes hadn't been closed for more than three minutes when her ears picked up a scraping sound coming from the hallway. Her eyes shot open as she twisted in her chair to peer toward the arched entry leading into the hall.

"Who's there?" she raised her voice nervously. "The tour is over. You better not have snuck from the group."

Never once, in all the years the haunted house had been in operation, had the Ungers not made sure the thirteen guests who entered the mansion had also exited. But in her haste that evening, Isabelle had neglected to take a head count of those leaving through the back door. One could have easily strayed from the group and hid among the various props within the mansion.

"Show yourself," Isabelle demanded, pushing herself to her feet. "I know you're out there."

She angrily stomped across the study toward the hall.

"Hold on, Vickie," Samara said, rubbing her arms. "Does anyone else feel that?"

"Feel what?" Vickie asked.

"It's like the temperature dropped. Do you think the furnace cut out?"

Darlene slowly strolled to the center of the floor, staring at Vickie. "It's not the furnace."

"Why are you staring at me when you say that?" Vickie asked.

Darlene grinned. "Some of us are naturally colder than others."

"What's that supposed to mean?"

"I think you know."

"Come on, guys," Samara jumped in, her voice now visible in the air. "Can we just calm down until Brandon gets back with help?"

"Where the hell is he, anyway?" Shawn spoke up.

"He'll be here," Chuck said. "They're probably on their way now. Can we just chill and let Vickie finish? I want to hear what happened."

"I can chill if *she* can chill," Vickie said, nodding toward Darlene.

"I can chill," Darlene responded with a curled lip. "Go on, then; finish your story."

Vickie squinted, displeased at Darlene, then looked back down at the page.

Isabelle stepped into the hall and turned to her left. The pale specter she saw was more than her heart could take. She gasped and clutched her chest, feeling her insides constrict until she couldn't breathe. Her legs buckled, and her knees slammed to the floor, her eyes bloodshot and still focused on the cause of her malady. Saliva leaked from the corner of her lips as she clenched her teeth. Veins bulged from her neck like they were about to explode. Then, her body slumped sideways, and she fell to the floor, motionless.

Everything was quiet. Nothing moved except the ominous phantom as it floated closer to the elderly woman's body.

A minute later, Isabelle picked herself up from the ground and dusted off the front of her clothes as if nothing had happened. She calmly walked to the front door, opened it with a smile, and allowed the next thirteen people to enter.

Vickie flipped the page but remained silent. Shawn licked his lips and leaned forward anxiously in the chair.

"And then what?"

"I don't know," Vickie said, staring at the page, shaking her head.

"What do you mean, you don't know?" Chuck questioned. "What's it say?"

"It's blank," Vickie answered.

She flipped several more pages. "They're all blank. There's nothing more."

Just then, the sound of a blood-curdling scream reverberated from upstairs.

"What the fuck was that?" Vickie questioned, slamming the book shut.

"Was that Jamie?" Samara asked, standing up, concern plastered on her face. "Something's wrong!"

"No way," Chuck answered with a smirk. "Pierce is up there with her. They're fucking around with us, trying to scare us."

Darlene stepped forward, "That's something *you* would do, Chuck, not Pierce, and definitely not Jamie."

Before any of them could contemplate their next move, the room's unbroken lamp flickered, causing them all to look in its direction. A second later, it flickered again as the soft hum of electricity waned with the dimming bulb. Then, the light went out, and the room fell silent.

Chapter 19

Jamie curled her legs up and pulled Pierce's arm over her like a blanket. She squeezed tighter to him, rubbing her butt against his crotch as they lay spooning. She felt the bulge in his pants shift and get hard, which brought a slight grin to her face. She remembered tender moments like this when they were a couple, how safe and warm Pierce would make her feel. They'd always been a perfect fit.

Until they weren't.

She blamed herself. It was *her* fault, the strain she had placed on their relationship. Pierce stood by her as long as he could, but she didn't make it easy for him. The battles in her head consumed her, which soon became battles with Pierce when he tried to rationalize with her. She should have listened to him. Instead, she pushed him away, like she did all her friends. Like she did to everyone.

When she looked back on that time in her life, she understood why they turned their back on her. They tried to help, but she thought they were against her, feeding her lies like she couldn't see through their deceit. They kept telling her it was all in her head, that it wasn't true, it wasn't real. But to her, the visions *were* real, and nothing they could say would make her believe otherwise.

Eventually, the doctors, the treatments, her stay in that awful facility.., they helped her distinguish between what was real and what was only a figment of her imagination. They helped her understand that it was her fears, her anxiety, and her overwhelming grief that caused the chemical imbalance in her brain to manifest visions of her dead parents and little brother, as if the car accident had never taken them from her. Once she accepted her new reality, that her life had been unmistakably and irreversibly altered in the worst possible way, the visions ceased to haunt her. The road to recovery hadn't been easy and had taken its toll, but it was something she had overcome. It was then up to her to mend the ties she'd severed along the way to her eventual breakdown. To recapture what she'd lost in her life. And, now that she'd gotten it back, she didn't want anything to take it away, especially not her overactive imagination.

Jamie gripped Pierce's arm tightly. "Thanks for being here," she said softly, enjoying the feel of his body against hers.

He didn't respond, but brought his lips closer to the back of her neck as his fingers subtly caressed the lower crease where her breast rested against her upper abdomen. He exhaled from his mouth, his breath wiggling stray strands of her hair against her neck, stimulating her and sending chills down her spine. Jamie closed her eyes and released her grip on his wrist, allowing it more freedom. His hand slid up until his palm cupped the lower portion of her breast. She felt her heart race excitedly. She felt his lips gently press against her skin, and then a tingling sensation between her legs, as his tongue moved in a circle just under her earlobe.

She licked her lips. "I know what you're trying to do. I'm okay with it if you want to."

She relaxed her shoulders and nuzzled her back into him, smiling at his actions. His index finger wandered up her breast to her nipple, having little trouble finding it poking through her shirt. As he twirled his finger around its base, Jamie quivered and inhaled deeply through her nose. Then, her eyes shot open, and a look of concern gripped her features.

"Do you smell that?" she questioned.

Pierce didn't reply as his tongue continued to swirl about the side of her neck.

"I'm serious." She inhaled a second time. "What is that? It's like rotting food."

She grabbed his arm to swing it off her so she could sit up, and that was when she noticed how cold his skin was.

"You're arm is like ice," she said, facing away from him as she swung her legs off the bed. "You should have said something. We could have gotten under the blanket."

She turned to face him with a contented smile on her face, and when she did, she almost fell to the floor trying to jump to her feet. She let out a scream as her body backed into the wall. She felt all the color leave her face as she stared at someone on the bed who was not Pierce. In his place was an older man with long scraggly hair, a gray mustache and goatee, and skin as pale as a white sheet. The man writhed on the bed, flicking his tongue out suggestively from blue-colored lips. His eyes were black like the boy she'd seen in the mirror. His light tan, buttoned shirt had several holes with fresh red stains seeping through the fabric around them. Jamie couldn't catch her breath. Adrenaline took over.

She turned and grabbed for the doorknob, but it wouldn't turn. She fumbled with it, shaking and tugging it in desperation.

"Come on," she said through gritted teeth. "Come on!"

When she realized the door wouldn't open, and her struggle was futile, she instinctively spun to face the strange man before he could grab her from behind.

Standing at the far side of the bed was Pierce, his eyes wide with fear and his mouth agape.

"What the hell, Jamie?"

"Where is he?" she yelled.

"Where is who? What are you talking about?"

"That man! He was right there on the bed." She pointed to the spot where, a minute before, she had been groped by a disgusting stranger.

"There's nobody here, Jamie," Pierce said, making his way around the bed. "I was with you on the bed when you suddenly screamed out and ran for the door."

"No, there was somebody else. I'm telling you, Pierce. He was touching me and licking my neck, and he smelled like he was..,"

"Like he was what?" Pierce asked, grabbing hold of her wrists.

"Like he was dead."

Pierce tilted his head to the side and exhaled from his nose, giving her a disappointed look.

"Not that again. Jamie, this has gotta..,"

The lights suddenly went out, leaving them in complete darkness.

"What's going on?" Jamie said with a quivering voice. She pulled her hands free from Pierce's hold and wrapped her arms around one of his biceps.

"I don't know. The power went out, or something."

"I want to get out of here, Pierce."

"Okay, okay. Let's go down with the others."

"The door won't open," Jamie said anxiously.

"What do you mean?" Pierce reached for the door and twisted the knob. The door creaked open. "It's open."

"I swear, it wouldn't open when I tried."

Disheartened, he exhaled through his nose. "Never mind; let's just get downstairs and find out what happened."

Chapter 20

The last sliver of light faded from the down-stairs window, leaving only darkness in its wake. The wind outside whistled as it shook the single-hung panes. And then, all was quiet for a brief moment until the flashlight on Chuck's phone lit up from under his chin, highlighting his face with distorted shadows.

"Boo!"

"Knock it off, Chuck," Pierce said, lighting his own phone's flashlight.

One after another, each phone flashed a beam of light to illuminate the room. All, save one.

"Sorry about your phone, Darlene," Samara said, turning her flashlight in her friend's direc-tion.

Darlene said nothing, having since resumed her spot by the window, peering out into the black void, seeing nothing past her reflection in the glass.

"Darlene?" Samara questioned.

Darlene swiveled her head to the left, just enough to see the group in her periphery.

"I like the dark."

"See?" Vickie chimed in. "That's what I'm talking about. She's acting crazy as fuck!"

"What did you say about me?" Darlene hissed through clenched teeth, turning fully to expose the discontent on her face.

"You heard me, bitch," Vickie growled back, stepping forward in a threatening manner.

"Can you two knock it off?" Jamie jumped in, stepping in front of Vickie to stop her progress. "We have more important things to work out than to keep you guys from chewing each other's asses."

"Like getting that tree removed," Shawn spoke up.

"Yeah," Pierce added. "Where the hell is Brandon anyway? Can somebody call him?"

"I've still got no service," Shawn responded.

"Nothing for me, either," Chuck said.

Samara followed with "Same."

"Oh, Jesus fucking Christ," Vickie announced heatedly, stepping by Jamie on her way to the hallway. "He's probably out by the tree now with some tree-removal company."

"Where are you going?" Jamie asked.

"I'm going to check if he's out there."

"You can't go out there alone," Pierce said.

Vickie stopped under the archway, turned, and gave Pierce a snide look.

"Don't worry, I wore big boy pants before I ever put on big girl pants."

She stepped past the threshold of the study into the hallway, entering the foyer, and her phone's light immediately cut out.

"Really? Ggrrrr! Fuck you!" She continued toward the front door, directed by the dim glow escaping the study's entrance. She could hear the others whispering their dissatisfaction, but she didn't care. She needed to get some fresh air, but mostly, she needed to get away from Darlene before she did something they'd both regret.

Agitated, Vickie stormed to the front door, twisted the knob, and yanked it open. Her eyes instantly expanded, and her jaw dropped, but she didn't have time to scream. She heard the thud of something hitting her chest before she registered the pain. Her fear-stricken face turned to confusion as she peered into the eyes of a white, featureless face, a mask with no nose, with a single drop of crimson below its white lips, traveling ever-so-slowly down its chin. Vickie stumbled back, trying to catch her breath, gurgling sounds emanating from her trembling lips. She looked down at the handle of a knife protruding from her chest, her blood seeping from the slice in her shirt. She looked up at the pale specter and coughed, red liquid spitting from her mouth.

"H-he-hel...," she murmured, her arms extended, unsuccessfully reaching for the figure before crumbling to the floor. Weak coughing overtook her words, speckling the wood floor in front of her face with droplets of blood. The noise was enough to alert her friends.

"What is she doing now?" Jamie questioned, walking to the edge of the study, followed closely by Pierce. When her light caught a glimpse of Vickie on the floor, lying on her side, she jumped into action.

"Oh my God! Vickie!" She sprinted to her friend's aid, unaware of the cause of her collapse. Just as Jamie approached, her shoes hit the blood spatter, causing her feet to slip out from under her. She tried twisting to catch herself, but landed hard on her hand, sending a jolt through her wrist.

"Jamie!" Pierce yelled, running to her side to check on her.

"I'm fine," she said, pushing herself up but feeling the liquid against her palm. "What the hell?" She turned her palm up as Pierce shone his light on her hand to reveal the blood dripping from it. Jamie's heart pounded, and her breath became shallow as her eyes shifted to Vickie. "Vickie?"

Pierce slowly turned his quavering hand toward their friend, the light first hitting Vickie's face, whose eyes peered at them with a vacant stare. His hand continued its motion until the source of the blood was revealed, spilling from the gaping wound in her chest where the knife had loosened upon her crashing to the floor. Jamie screamed and pushed herself back from the body, trying to get to her feet but landing on her butt.

"What the fuck?" Pierce yelled. "What the fuck? She's dead!" he cried out, the rest of the group frozen with fear as they looked on from the archway. "Somebody did this." He immediately looked to the open door and ran out onto the porch. "Who did this?" he screamed, waving his light from side to side into the darkness, hoping to catch movement.

Samara ran into the foyer to help Jamie to her feet, while Chuck ran past them and out the door.

"Come on, Jamie; I've got you," Samara said, pulling her up by her armpit, tears beginning to leak from the corner of her eyes.

Jamie tensed, trying to pull away, but Samara held firm. "What if she's still alive? What if..?"

"She's not," Darlene said coldly from beside Shawn in the study's doorway.

"You don't know that," Jamie yelled, flailing her arm, struggling to free herself.

"She's dead, Jamie," Samara stated, dragging her into the study.

Outside, Chuck joined Pierce at the edge of the top step of the porch.

"What the fuck is going on, man?" Chuck questioned with fear in his voice, waving his own light into the dirt driveway.

"I don't know."

"What just happened?"

"I don't know."

"Who the fuck did that?"

"I don't know!" Pierce screamed, slamming his palm against the porch's railing. "What do you want from me? Jesus Christ, I don't know! Do you see anybody?"

"No, I don't see anybody. Fuck! Should we go looking?"

"No. I don't know. We've gotta call the police. What if whoever did this has a gun?"

"Oh shit! We've gotta get back in the house." Chuck grabbed Pierce's arm and backed up toward the front door.

"But what if the person is out here? They could be hiding behind one of the cars."

"You just said they could have a gun," Chuck argued.

"But what if they don't? We can't let the fucker get away with this."

"They won't," Chuck bellowed, continuing to tug on his friend's arm. "We'll call the police. They'll catch the son of a bitch. But we've gotta get inside. Let's go!"

Reluctantly, Pierce took a step back, continuing to wave his light from side to side. Feeling his friend's wavering resolve, Chuck pulled a little harder, spinning Pierce around.

"Let's go!" Chuck repeated, pulling him through the front door before slamming it shut and locking the deadbolt.

They lumbered past Vickie, their eyes trained on her motionless body, the painted fake blood on the floor being flooded by the real liquid.

They stepped into the study to see Samara and Darlene consoling Jamie on the sofa. Samara and Jamie were holding each other, crying. Darlene held Jamie's hand, no tears in her eyes. Shawn stood over them awkwardly, holding his hand over his mouth as if unsure how to act around the three women.

"Did someone call 911?" Chuck said anxiously, steering Pierce toward the wingback chair.

They all looked at him in shock, as if wondering why they hadn't already thought of that.

"Shit!" Chuck said, forcing Pierce into the chair. "I've got it."

He turned his screen up to press the emergency button, but his light flickered just before the phone went dead.

"No, no, no. Come on. Fuck."

Shawn raised his phone to dial, but it, too, turned black.

"Guys, what is going on?" he said.

A third light went out as Pierce's phone died, followed by Samara's, leaving only Jamie's beam of light, shooting up from her lap to the ceiling.

"Jamie," Samara said, her voice shaking nervously, "yours is still working. Quick, call!"

Jamie quickly snatched her phone, turned it over, and the light went out.

Chapter 21

A chill swept into the darkened room. Jamie and Samara's tears dried on their tacky cheeks as sorrow gave way to fear. For a moment, everything remained silent in the blackness save for the six friends' heavy breathing. And then, like a freight train passing in the night, the silence was broken.

"What the hell is going on here, guys?" Chuck questioned. The fear was heavily present in his voice.

Jamie squeezed Samara and Darlene's hands tighter. "Pierce?" she whimpered.

"I'm here," he replied from the chair in the center of the room. "Everybody, just keep calm. We'll figure this out."

"Flashlight," Jamie said, as the idea suddenly popped into her head.

"What?"

"I have a flashlight in my car."

"That's just great," Chuck replied snidely. "That does us a whole lot of good in here."

"We can go and get it," Jamie said quietly, brushing off his comment.

"Out there?" Chuck questioned brusquely. "Outside is where whoever did that to Vickie is." In his excitement, he shifted forward and banged his shin on the coffee table. "Ouch! Fuck!"

"Chuck?" Samara cried out. She released Jamie's hand and reached forward to feel for him.

"I'm fine. I just banged my leg on the table."

"Jamie's right," Pierce stated. "We need to get the flashlight out of her car."

"Are you crazy?" Chuck raised his voice. "Our friend is dead! Someone out there killed her, and you want to go traipsing out there in the dark?"

"We have to try," Pierce responded. "We can't just sit here in the dark doing nothing."

Samara jumped in, "Maybe it won't be long. Brandon will be back soon with help."

"What if Brandon's not coming back?" Shawn said.

"He's always been weird," Chuck replied, "but he wouldn't take off and leave us stranded."

"I didn't mean it that way," Shawn answered. "I meant, what if whoever killed Vickie also killed Brandon?"

Just then, Darlene started rocking back and forth on the sofa, mumbling the words to a song.

"Baby, won't you please come home?"

"What the hell are you doing, Darlene?" Chuck questioned. "This isn't a joke."

Darlene didn't answer, but continued her strange behavior of rocking and singing.

"Baby, won't you please come home?"

"What the fuck?" Chuck added, agitated.

Jamie threw her arm over Darlene's shoulder to comfort her.

"Never mind her," Pierce said. "And Brandon is fine, Shawn. I watched him ride off down the driveway. He'll be back."

"Then why isn't he back already?" Shawn continued.

"Jesus Christ, Shawn!" Pierce shouted. "Shut up, already."

"Baby, won't you please come home?"

"Oh my God," Chuck yelled out heatedly. "I can't deal with this. I'll go out for the flashlight. I'd rather take my chances out there than listen to this shit."

"Will you guys stop it!" Jamie yelled. "You're freaking her out."

"She's freaking *me* out," Chuck responded.

"Baby, won't you please come..,"

And then the mansion's lights flashed back on, instantly ending Darlene's incessant rocking and singing.

"Oh, thank God!" Samara said, placing her hand on her chest to ensure her heart was still beating.

"My phone is still dead," Shawn said, looking at his screen.

The rest quickly looked at their phones and saw he wasn't alone.

"That's another reason we should go for the flashlight," Pierce said. "Something in this house is affecting our phones. Maybe they'll work outside."

"The outside lights on the porch should be working," Chuck added. "If we go together, we can watch each other's backs."

"What about Vickie?" Samara asked, holding back renewed tears. "We can't just leave her in the foyer like that."

"We have to," Jamie said. "It's a crime scene."

"Can we at least cover her up?"

"I think so. We should grab her blanket."

"Okay, you girls do that," Pierce said. "Chuck and I will go for the flashlight."

"What about me?" Shawn asked.

Pierce looked over at Darlene, who sat motionless. Her eyes were glossed over like she was in shock.

"You keep watch over Darlene."

Shawn nodded.

"All right; are we ready?" Pierce questioned confidently.

"Wait!" Jamie shouted. She got up from the sofa and ran out into the hallway and toward the kitchen. A moment later, she returned with two knives. "Here." She handed them to Chuck and Pierce.

"Butter knives?" Chuck questioned.

"I don't know; I just grabbed, okay?"

Pierce tapped his knife against Chuck's and shrugged his shoulders. "It's better than nothing. Let's go."

"Why don't I just grab that one?" Chuck said, pointing at the bloody knife in Vickie's chest.

"No!" Jamie said with a raised voice. "The police will need that. It could have fingerprints on it."

Chuck looked down at the butter knife he was holding and shook his head. Pierce recognized the look and quickly grabbed his attention.

"Chuck, we'll be all right. There are two of us. If someone's out there, we have each other's backs."

"And if the fucker has a gun?"

Everyone went silent. Pierce looked down at Vickie's body, then back to his friend.

"Then that knife wouldn't do you any good, anyway."

Pierce looked at Jamie and nodded, giving her a half-hearted smile.

"Come on, Samara," Jamie said. She tugged at Samara's hand to follow her upstairs. Samara made it to the second tread before turning.

"Be careful, Chuck."

He smiled. "I'm always careful."

Jamie and Samara continued up the staircase to Vickie's room. Chuck and Pierce slowly made their way around Vickie's bloody corpse, keeping their eyes glued to her until they reached the door. Chuck flipped the light switch to the porch lights on while Pierce unlocked the door's deadbolt and grabbed the knob. He looked at Chuck and took three quick breaths.

"Are you ready?"

Chuck nodded, nervously staring at him.

Pierce gave the knob a quick twist, but it didn't turn.

"What?" he whispered to himself.

He tried again, but the knob wouldn't turn.

"Open the door," Chuck said.

"It won't open. The knob is stuck." He grabbed it with both hands and jiggled it, trying to wrestle it open.

"Let *me* give it a try," Chuck said.

Pierce backed away, giving Chuck a chance. Chuck grabbed the knob with both hands, but was met with the same unsatisfactory result.

"What the fuck?" Chuck yelled. "We just had it open a little while ago."

"What's wrong?" Jamie said from the top of the staircase. She and Samara were making their way down with a light blue blanket in hand.

"The door won't open," Pierce answered. His voice cracked with frustration.

"What do you mean, it won't open?"

"I mean, it won't open. The knob is stuck. We can't get out."

"What about the back door?" Jamie asked.

Chuck and Pierce turned their stare to each other, a look of worry in their eyes.

"What?" Jamie asked. "What's wrong?"

Chuck swallowed heavily, turning back to her. "Doesn't the back door lead out into the cemetery?"

Chapter 22

Jamie and Samara stared into their friend's lifeless eyes, holding back tears, as Jamie pulled the edge of the blanket up over Vickie's face. The pooled blood on the floor seeped into the fabric, quickly spreading upward along Vickie's chest.

"Why would somebody do this?" Samara asked, standing over her friend.

"I don't know," Jamie replied. She pushed herself up from a squatted position. "I can't think about that right now. I just want to get out of here."

"I know. Where the hell is Brandon?"

"He's not coming," a voice spoke behind them, causing them to jump. It was Shawn, standing under the arch of the study's doorway.

Jamie exhaled from her nose, discontented at his comment. "Shut the hell up, Shawn!"

"I don't like to think it, either," He responded. "But if Brandon were coming back, he would have been here already."

"You don't know that," Samara argued.

"You're right; I don't. But something doesn't feel right."

"*Nothing* about this feels right," Jamie said. "One of our friends is dead, our phones keep cutting in and out, and we're trapped in this goddamn house." She crossed her arms about her chest and stormed toward the study, stopping by Shawn's side to look him in the eyes with a glare that burned through him. "You saying all this negative shit isn't helping anybody." She continued past him to check on Darlene.

He turned his eyes toward Samara, who had a dour look on her face. "I'm sorry," he said. Samara shook her head and walked by him, joining the other two women in the study.

At the rear of the house, in a small mudroom, Pierce stared at the back door, its solid oak wood finish faded with age. There were no windows to look through, only a small sign affixed to the door that read, "Thank you for coming. Have a nice fright." The room, located down a narrow hallway off the kitchen, was uncharacteristically small compared to the rest of the rooms they'd seen. They'd passed by a half bath in the hallway that was even smaller and smelled like the septic had backed up. Chuck had taken a quick glance on his way by, contemplating using it since his nerves had made his insides stir, but the smell alone was enough to deter him. That, and the thought of wedging himself into a claustrophobic space in a house where doors seemed to mysteriously prevent people from escaping, was particularly unappealing.

The one promising thing was that they had passed through the kitchen on their way to the rear exit, which allowed them to trade in their insufficient butter knives for utensils that were a bit more intimidating.

Pierce unlatched the slide mechanism that was keeping the door locked and stared intently at his friend. Chuck squeezed the butcher knife in his fist and nodded. Pierce looked down at his own weapon, a small meat cleaver that had seen better days, the metal along its bladed edge chipped in several locations.

"Here we go," he muttered softly as the knob spun in his hand. The door opened only a crack, enough to let them know they could exit. Sucking in a heavy amount of air, Pierce gave a sharp tug, swinging the door open wide, while the two of them simultaneously raised their weapons threateningly, anticipating having to use them.

A subtle breeze swept into the doorway as the two stared out upon an empty cemetery. The dim glow of an overhead floodlight, mounted high above the rear door, cascaded across the head-stones, casting extended shadows to the lip of the field beyond. Dense fog hung over the tall grass, slowly creeping into the cemetery, mingling with the gravestones of the fictitiously departed.

The rear door hadn't opened onto a porch, like along the front of the mansion, but instead, to a four-foot square concrete patio at ground level. At the front of the small landing, a trail of brick-colored pavers snaked its way through the tiny graveyard toward the side of the house. Weeds shot up from between every available crevice, overtaking the path in a lush green hue.

Chuck let out a sigh of relief while keeping his words just above a whisper.

"I don't see anyone, do you?"

Pierce shifted his eyes left, then right. "No."

"I think we can make it."

"All right. But we've gotta go quietly."

Chuck nodded, stepping through the door first, his eyes wide, sweeping across the cemetery. He froze at the edge of the overgrown pathway, waiting for Pierce to join him. Pierce stepped out from the open door and nudged Chuck's left shoulder.

"Let's go."

"Yeah. Stay close."

Chuck edged forward onto the pavers, shuf-fling slowly along the pathway, feeling Pierce's presence hovering close behind him. As they wandered through the thickening haze dancing across their knees, they listened for any sound or unnatural movement that wasn't their own. Chuck swung his head from side to side, staying alert, occasionally flinching at the sound of their feet scraping across the concrete pathway. He found himself casually glancing at some of the stone markers along the way as a distraction to keep his fear from growing. Suddenly, he froze when one of the gravestones on his left caught his eye. He stiffened and lowered his brow in confusion.

"What the fuck?" he blurted.

"Chuck!" Pierce stated, to no response.

Chuck stood in stunned silence, staring and pointing at the stone that had grabbed his attention.

"Chuck!" Pierce yelled louder, yanking on his friend's sleeve.

Chuck turned his wide-eyed stare to Pierce, who pointed ahead of them toward the rear corner of the house. He swiveled around to see an ominous figure, standing at attention, his feet shoulder-distance apart. From the floodlight's glow, it appeared to be a man wearing white coveralls, his arms crossed behind his back. He wore a smooth white mask with darkened eyes, white lips, and no nose. Chuck felt himself swallow hard, and his heart beat faster. The figure remained still, peering at them through the mask's black eyes.

"What do you want?" Pierce shouted.

The man in the mask stood firm.

"The police are on their way," Chuck added.

Still, the masked figure stood his ground, remaining silent.

"We have weapons!" Pierce yelled. "We don't want to hurt you, but we will."

The figure in white leaned his head first to his left shoulder, and then to his right, like he was cracking his neck. When he brought his head straight, he pulled his hands from behind his back to reveal a machete in his right hand.

"Oh shit!" Pierce mumbled.

Chuck glanced down at the knife he wielded and tightened his forearm. Keeping his eyes trained on the threatening figure, he turned his head slightly to speak over his shoulder.

"I think we can take him."

"What?" Pierce questioned. "What the fuck are you talking about?"

Without explaining, Chuck yelled to the masked man, "We're not afraid of you, dipshit! There are two of us and only *one* of you."

With those words, the figure methodically turned his head to his right and then back to them. Chuck and Pierce glanced diagonally to their left to see what had his attention. There, shrouded in thick fog, just past the cemetery at the edge of the field, stood a second figure, dressed in the same mask and white garb as the first. Like the threatening figure before them, this man carried a weapon in his right hand, as well: a small hatchet.

"Oh fuck! Oh fuck!" Pierce cried out. "We've gotta get back in the house."

Keeping their eyes forward, they slowly backed up, kicking away the weeds along the hard surface. The two masked men turned their heads to each other, nodded, and then sprinted forward after their prey.

"Shit!" Chuck yelled. "Go! Go!"

They clumsily turned on their heels and ran for the open rear door. Pierce made it to the concrete pad when he heard a thud behind him. He turned to see Chuck on the ground, his foot tangled in some weeds that cluttered the path. Pierce took a step toward his fallen friend. "Chuck!" he cried, but it was too late. One of the two men in white stood over Chuck's writhing body as he tried to free himself of the overgrown weeds. When the figure raised the machete high overhead, Pierce dove through the open door and slammed it shut behind him. He sat on the floor with his back pressed against the door, listening to his friend's anguished screams until they faded into silence. He sat for a moment, unmoving, staring down the narrow hallway, hearing only his shallow breathing. He reached up with his left hand and slid the door's latch to the locked position.

Chapter 23

Darlene sat at the end of the sofa, gently rubbing her fingers across the cover of the book she'd taken from the end table. She began humming while staring blankly at the picture of Reaper House on its face. Jamie sat beside her, rubbing Darlene's arm, occasionally glancing at Samara, who was leaning her shoulder into the mantle above the fireplace with her arms folded across her chest.

"It's going to be all right, Darlene," Jamie said.

Darlene continued humming without acknowledging her friend. Jamie looked at Samara again, who raised her eyebrows and shook her head.

"What's wrong with her, anyway?" Shawn asked, as if he didn't feel Darlene was present enough to answer the question herself. "Why is she acting that way? None of the rest of us are out of our minds," he spoke out of turn, irritating Jamie and Samara.

"I think she's in shock," Jamie scowled. She tucked strands of hair that were hanging down the side of Darlene's cheek over her ear. Darlene didn't react, only continued staring at the book's cover.

Samara spoke up. "I think she's taking Vickie's death harder because they got into an argument before, you know.., *it* happened. She probably feels guilty."

Just then, Darlene's humming stopped. She shifted her eyes from the book to Samara and spoke in a calm, slow voice. "Is that what you think, little girl?"

Feeling uncomfortable with Darlene's comment, Samara pushed herself upright and dropped her arms to her sides, swallowing heavily. "I just..."

"The reaper came for her," Darlene cut her off. She looked back at the book. "The reaper comes for us all."

"What are you talking about?" Jamie questioned in a concerned tone. "What's going on with you?"

Shawn took a few steps away from the sofa, dividing his time between looking at Samara and then at the two women on the couch.

"You should read the book," Darlene said, tapping her fingernails on the cover.

Jamie turned her wide-eyed stare to Samara and silently mouthed the words "What the fuck?"

Darlene repeated, "You should read the book."

"I don't want to read the book," Jamie stated angrily. "Our friend is dead. Don't you care?" She turned to Samara, looking for guidance. "Samara?"

Samara shrugged. "Anyway," she began, "Vickie already read some of it while you were upstairs with Pierce. She stopped when she got to the blank pages."

Darlene suddenly burst out laughing, causing Jamie to slide away from her in shock. Then, just as quickly, the laughing ceased.

"They're not blank anymooorree," Darlene said, drawing out the last syllable like she was channeling the little girl from Poltergeist. "Read it!" She slid the book off her lap onto the cushion between them.

Jamie gazed at her friend, whose eyes remained focused down on her empty lap. Then, Jamie shifted her stare to the book and let out a frustrated breath. She felt a tingling down her spine as she reached for it and crouched her neck into her shoulders to relieve her nerves. She pulled the book onto her lap, flipped it open to a random page in the middle, and began reading aloud.

Taking the woman's life was easier than expected, the way her neck twisted abnormally about her spine. She dropped to the hardwood floor, nearly tumbling down the stairs. That would have been problematic. The noise would have alerted the others. Isabelle grabbed the woman's ankles and quickly slid her across the floor to the hidden cubby in the wall across from the bathroom. Nobody would find her there.

"What page is that?" Shawn interrupted.

"156," Jamie replied.

Samara pointed at the page from her position by the fireplace. "Th-that wasn't there before. Those pages were blank."

"There are words on them now," Jamie stated. "Are you sure they were all blank?"

"Keep reading," Darlene whispered without looking away from her lap.

Jamie looked back at the book and flipped several more pages.

She held the plastic bag over his head long after he had expired, taking delight in her work. During his asphyxiation, his lips had changed from dark red to pale white to blue, and finally, a dark purple. She left him lying on the bathroom floor when she exited.

Jamie's thoughts jumped to the vision of the boy she'd seen in the bathroom mirror. She knew it must have been him. The words gave her chills.

She flipped past several more pages, hoping to get beyond the chilling murders.

The knife went in cleanly when the girl turned her back. Her screams went unheard, as she was the last to fall.

Jamie slammed the book shut. "I can't. I can't read anymore." She tossed it onto the coffee table in front of her, and it slid to the far edge. Shawn snatched it up, opened deeper into the book, and read from a page.

And then they came to disturb the silence, the group of eight plus three. Their arrival had put an end to the long slumber. The two had returned, and in doing so, had sealed their fate. The reaper had been summoned, once again, to take what was due. Vengeance will not rest until the last one has fallen. Let the silencing begin.

"Ooooo, scary," Shawn said facetiously, wiggling his fingers jokingly. "What does any of that even mean?"

"A group of eight plus three?" Samara questioned. "Why not just say eleven?"

Darlene looked up from her lap, smiled at Samara, and spouted in a deep, raspy voice, "Eight,

eight, eight, eight, eight, eight, eight, eight, plus three, three, three."

Samara shook her head and slapped her thigh. "What is she going on about? Like seriously."

Jamie's eyes looked past Darlene into the foyer, where she could see the edge of the light-blue blanket covering Vickie's body. Her thoughts went to the knife sticking out of her chest. It was clear someone had stabbed her.

"A group of eight plus three," she murmured.

"What?" Samara questioned.

"Guys, *we* came as a group of eight."

"Yeah. So?" Shawn said.

"So, what if we're the eight the book is referring to?"

"That's ridiculous," Shawn replied. "How can the book have things written about us?"

"Samara said the pages were blank before, right?"

"So what?"

"Now they're not. Don't you think that's strange? It's like new stuff has been added."

"Okay, that's weird," Samara said. "But still, it said eight plus three. So, it can't be about us."

Jamie looked back into the foyer. "Unless..,"

Just then, Pierce stepped into the arched opening from the hallway, a look of dread on his face.

Jamie jumped up from the couch and ran to him.

"Thank God, you're back." She wrapped her arms around him and immediately noticed how rigid he was. She pulled away. "Did you get the flashlight?"

Pierce's mouth opened, but nothing came out as his eyes shifted between the four in the room.

"What's wrong?" Jamie asked.

Then Samara jumped in. "Pierce?" she questioned, wide-eyed. "Where's Chuck?"

Chapter 24

No words could convey the message Pierce's face had already expressed. His eyes were an open book, his tears, the flowing ink on the page. He stumbled into the study near collapse, his eyes bloodshot, his cheeks red where he'd furiously wiped them. With utter remorse, he gazed at Samara for several seconds before dropping his chin to his chest.

Samara stood silent, her eyes swelling with salty liquid.

"No, no, no, no." She shook her head from side to side in disbelief. "Pierce, no. He's right behind you. Tell me Chuck's right behind you."

"I...I," Pierce's words faded to silence.

Samara's shoulders slumped, shortening her already diminutive frame. "Nooo!" She screamed. Tears streamed from her eyes like waterfalls as she lost feeling in her legs and tumbled forward into

Shawn's saving arms. "Chuck! No!" she cried, pushing herself clear of Shawn's chest.

"Samara," Pierce began, heavy-hearted, "there wasn't anything..,"

"Fuck you, Pierce!" Samara screamed with rage through the falling tears. "He's out there. We have to help him." She darted for the hallway with fierce determination, but Pierce threw out his arm and caught her before she left the study. "Let go of me!" she screamed, slamming her fists repeatedly into his arms and chest. "He needs my help! He needs my help. He needs..,"

"He's gone, Samara," Pierce said in a quiet, somber tone, squeezing her tightly in his arms.

Her body went limp, no longer able to stand on her own. She broke down in uncontrollable sobbing, gasping for breath between fits of coughing. Pierce looked at Jamie over Samara's high tuft of hair and subtly shook his head. She stepped forward and gently grabbed Samara's arm, pulling her from Pierce to sit her down on the sofa before she collapsed under the weight of her sorrow. Darlene slid over to give her room.

Jamie sat Samara down, rubbing her upper back and shoulders while she fought back tears of her own, trying to remain strong for both of them.

"Did you see who did it?" Jamie asked, turning her eyes to Pierce while consoling her friend.

With a quivering voice, Pierce spoke. "They were out there. They waited for us. We ran back, but Chuck tripped behind me. By the time I turned, one of them was already standing over him. There was nothing I could do. They would have killed us both."

"How many?" Jamie asked.

"What?"

"How many of them were there?"

"I heard his screams," Pierce said, ignoring her words. "I couldn't save him."

"Pierce!" she yelled.

Shawn reeled in surprise while Darlene sat quietly beside Samara, staring at the book in Shawn's hand.

"How many?" Jamie questioned again more firmly.

"Two," Pierce answered. "There were two."

"Three," Darlene mumbled.

"What?" Jamie questioned, turning her stare to Darlene.

Maintaining her blank stare, Darlene muttered, "Eight plus three."

Pierce shook his head. "There were only two."

"Are you sure?" Jamie asked.

"I'm telling you, there were only two. Fuck, I was out there."

"Eight plus three," Darlene repeated, almost singing the words. "*Eight plus three. They came to disturb the silence. The two had returned. Vengeance will not rest.*"

"What is going on here?" Pierce asked. "What the hell is she talking about.

"It's nothing," Shawn jumped in. "She's quoting from the book." He waved the book in the air in front of his chest. "She's obviously in shock."

Darlene's eyes shifted up from the book to meet Shawn's. "Eight. Plus. Three." Her voice was deep and hoarse.

"What is wrong with her?" Pierce asked.

"Shut up!" Samara yelled, holding her stomach and rocking back and forth. "All of you, shut up!"

Jamie squatted beside her and placed her hands on Samara's lap.

"Samara," she began softly, "I know it's hard. We all loved Chuck. Vickie, too. But there are people out there who are trying to kill us. We need to be strong right now and think of a way out of here. Can you do that? Can you keep it together?"

Samara bit back hard on the tears, trembling and compressing her stomach with her forearms like she was trying to keep from vomiting. Her lips quivered as she stared into Jamie's eyes and nodded.

"Okay," Jamie said, rubbing Samara's thighs. She stood and turned toward Pierce. "There were two of them?" she questioned.

"Yeah, two of them," he replied.

"Are you sure there wasn't a third?"

"Yeah, I'm sure. Why do you keep asking me?"

Darlene snapped her head sideways. "Eight plus three."

"Okay, what is up with her?" Pierce asked, pointing. "She's acting psycho. What is eight plus three?"

Jamie exhaled. "It's from the book. Something strange is going on around here, and apparently, there are now written pages that used to be blank. One of the passages stated something about people arriving here and disturbing the silence. A group of eight plus three. I mentioned that *we* came as a group of eight, and now, it's in all of our heads. If we're the eight, then maybe there are three others?"

"Are you serious?" Pierce questioned heatedly. "My best friend - Samara's boyfriend - was just killed. Vickie was stabbed. And you think some book I just pulled out of the library this morning is telling you a story about us? About what's going on right now?"

"You're right," Jamie agreed. "It's ridiculous. Let's just forget about that and concentrate on what we need to do. You said there were two of them?"

"Yes. One had a machete, the other a hatchet."

"Did you get a good look at them?"

"They were wearing masks. These white masks that looked like a face, only without a nose."

"White masks. A machete and a hatchet," Shawn repeated. "Great. We're being stalked by Jason Voorhees wannabes."

"They weren't hockey masks," Pierce retorted.

"I was obviously joking," Shawn replied.

"Doesn't matter," Jamie said. "They're out there, and they have weapons. We need to stay in here and stick together. If we do that, we can make it until Brandon comes back with help."

"I'm telling you, he's not coming back," Shawn blurted.

"Shut up, Shawn!" Samara yelled. "He'll be here."

Shawn shook his head, frustrated.

"Listen," Jamie said forcefully. "As long as they don't get in, we're safe."

"They could easily break a window," Pierce said.

"Then why haven't they? Jamie questioned. "If they wanted to, they would have done that already. They're playing with us. They want us scared. They want us to stay inside. They're herding us. If we go out, we're dead."

"And if you're wrong?" Shawn questioned. "If they decide they want in?"

"Well, that's why we need to stick together. There are five of us, and only two of them."

"Eight plus three, three, three," Darlene spewed.

"Okay, will somebody shut her up?" Pierce barked. "I told you there were only two."

Suddenly, a loud banging erupted from down the hall toward the kitchen.

"What was that?" Shawn shouted, his eyes stretched open. "Did you guys hear that?"

Darlene shifted her eyes toward the arched doorway and whispered, "Eight plus three."

Chapter 25

All eyes were focused out into the hallway. Jamie was sure her heart was beating through her chest as loudly as the sound they'd all heard from elsewhere on the first floor. Her breathing shallowed as she thought of Darlene's repetitive chants. *Eight plus three.* A warning, perhaps, transcribed in the pages of a book, foretelling an ominous threat yet to come. Or has it arrived already?

"You all heard that, right?" Pierce questioned, looking at the others.

Shawn nodded, his mouth agape.

"Yeah," Jamie replied.

"Uh-huh," Samara answered, wiping away tears from her chapped cheeks.

Darlene remained silent, curling her upper lip into a smirk as her eyes darted from person to person, surveying their reactions.

"Someone should check it out," Pierce said. He stepped toward the study's arched entryway before Jamie stopped him.

"Wait!" She grabbed his forearm to halt him. "We should all go together."

"I'm not going out there," Samara said with a fear-stricken voice.

Jamie turned to her with sympathetic eyes. "Samara, we need to stick together. If there's..."

"I said, I'm not going out there!" Her words were stern, her demeanor far stronger than her five-foot stature conveyed.

Jamie let out a disappointed breath from her nose.

"It's okay," Pierce said. "You stay here with Samara. Shawn, Darlene, and I can check it out." He glanced over at Darlene, who stared at him with a glossed-over glare, shaking her head. "Okay, Shawn and I will check it out."

"We will?" Shawn questioned, swallowing down the lump that had formed in his throat.

"Yes. We're *both* going."

"This is a very bad idea," Shawn offered, shaking his head while handing Jamie the book he was holding.

"If there *is* somebody in the house," Pierce began, "we can't just sit here and wait for them to come for us."

"The reaper comes for us all," Darlene interjected, her voice sounding as far away as her stare.

"Jesus Christ, Darlene!" Pierce yelled. "Fuck! I don't know what is wrong with you, but we don't need that shit right now."

"Okay, calm down," Jamie stated. She patted her empty hand in the air in front of her.

"No, she seriously needs to pull her shit together."

"I'll talk with her, but yelling at her isn't going to help."

Pierce closed his eyes in frustration and rubbed his forehead. "Okay. Sorry. I'm just a little stressed right now."

"I know you are," Jamie affirmed. "We *all* are. But you've gotta keep your head."

Pierce stared into her eyes, pursed his lips, and nodded his acceptance.

Jamie turned her head to Shawn. "Are you ready?"

His eyes shifted to the cleaver Pierce was holding. "I don't have a weapon."

Pierce gripped the cleaver tighter in his hand. "You can stay behind me."

"Now *that's* a good idea," Shawn responded, pointing at Pierce.

"All right, let's go." Pierce nodded his head sideways toward the hallway, but before he could lead the way, Jamie grabbed his arm again, stopping him.

"Pierce."

He looked her in the eyes and could see the overwhelming worry. He was about to lie to her and tell her everything was going to be all right, but before he could get the words out, Jamie stepped closer to him, grabbed both sides of his face, and pulled him into a kiss.

Shawn averted his eyes as if slightly embarrassed. Samara's lips quivered as snot ran down from her nose. It took everything she had not to break down in hysterics, as her thoughts jumped to Chuck and how much she enjoyed kissing him.

Jamie pulled away from Pierce, her eyes telling him everything he needed to know. He grinned.

"That would have been better if you hadn't had the book pressed against my cheek."

She faked a smile. "Sorry. Be careful."

"I will. Don't worry; I'll come back to you." He glanced at Shawn. "Let's go."

Pierce led the way into the hall as Shawn waddled along behind him. He paused for a moment to look at Vickie's covered body, the blanket now soaked in blood. Then, he turned toward the stretch of hallway leading to the kitchen, where the loud noise came from. "Stay close," he said in a hushed tone.

"Oh, you don't have to worry about that," Shawn whispered back.

They edged their way down the hall, keeping their backs pressed against the wall opposite the staircase, occasionally looking behind them. Pierce would initiate the look back, followed by Shawn, as if he felt he needed to mimic Pierce's moves. They continued sliding along until they were facing a door across from them, behind the staircase. It was the room that Shawn and Brandon were first assigned, where Shawn cut himself on the mechanical surgeon's razor-sharp scalpel. Pierce squinted, trying to gaze into the darkened room from across the hall, but couldn't see past the veil of blackness. He put his head down, listening for any unusual sounds. When he didn't hear anything, he glanced to his left, where, another twenty feet ahead, was the entrance to the kitchen. He nudged Shawn with his elbow.

"What do you think?" he whispered, nodding toward the darkened room in front of them.

Shawn responded by shaking his head negatively. Pierce then bobbed his head sideways toward the kitchen. Shawn gulped, but then responded with an accepting nod of his own.

"Okay," Pierce whispered. He brought his index finger to his mouth, signaling Shawn to keep silent. Shawn agreed.

They inched closer to the kitchen entrance. Pierce adjusted the cleaver in his sweaty grip while Shawn looked over his shoulder into the lighted room. Pierce looked back at him and waved his hand forward as if to say, *"We're going in."* He looked back at the kitchen doorway, clutched the cleaver tightly, and jumped forward into the entrance like he thought he might surprise a would-be assailant. His grip on the weapon loosened when he saw that the kitchen was empty. Shawn hurried forward into the space to stay as close to Pierce as he could.

"Thank goodness," Shawn whispered, breathing heavily.

Pierce couldn't tell if Shawn's labored breathing was from fear or if he was out of breath from bounding forward as quickly as he had. Pierce pointed across the kitchen to the back hallway.

"That leads to the rear door," he said quietly.

"Did you lock it?" Shawn asked.

"Yes." He paused for a moment, then added with a hint of doubt in his voice, "I'm pretty sure I did, anyway. You stay here; I'll go take a look."

"You won't get an argument from me."

Pierce strode forward less cautiously toward the rear hallway until he reached the far wall just before the rear kitchen doorway. He leaned his back against the wall, looked at Shawn, then turned and darted across the threshold into the hall, similarly to how he entered the kitchen. This time, however, his eyes widened, and fear gripped his face.

"Shit!" he yelled. "They're at the back door trying to get in." He turned his head to Shawn. "Get the girls and see if you can get out. I'll hold them off." He charged forward, disappearing out of Shawn's sight.

Shawn felt his shoulders tense as fear urged him backward and out of the kitchen. He turned and rushed as quickly as his massive frame could carry him back toward the study. Just as he passed by the room at the rear of the staircase, white leather-gloved hands whipped out of the darkness, holding a strand of barbed wire. The wire swung over Shawn's head and wrapped around his neck, the barbs puncturing his skin and jerking his head back. A white-masked figure emerged from the room and tugged on the wire, squeezing it ever tighter. The barbs dug deeper into Shawn's flesh with every movement he made as he brought his hands up to his neck, trying to relieve the pressure. The figure clad in white pulled harder, causing Shawn to lose his footing and stumble backward into the dark embrace of the room. Strained gurgling sounds soon gave way to a thud.

And then, silence.

Chapter 26

Samara sat with her hands on her lap, her fingers intertwined, as she nervously bounced her legs up and down. She'd held back the tears, her bouts of grief quickly wiped away by the fear of her and her friends' present situation.

"I can't believe this is happening," she said, staring down at her hands, afraid to look up. "Why is this happening? Who's doing this?"

"I don't know," Jamie answered in a troubled tone. She looked at her phone, its face still displaying a blank screen. She huffed in frustration, dropping her hand to her side. She paced across the room, swinging the book in her hand as she trodded back and forth, the cover rubbing against her pant leg. She glanced sideways at Darlene, whose uncomfortable stare made her feel uneasy.

"What?" Jamie hissed, stopping in her tracks. "What are you staring at?"

Samara looked up to see who Jamie was talking to, and then over at Darlene at the other end of the sofa. Darlene remained silent, stiff, unfazed by Jamie's outburst. Then, slowly, she raised her left arm from her side and extended it forward, pointing at the book Jamie held.

Jamie looked down at her hand. "What? The book? You want the fucking book?" she seethed. "Here, take the goddamn book." She angrily tossed the book forward onto the couch between the other two women, nearly striking Darlene with it. Samara reeled from Jamie's reaction, but Darlene didn't flinch. "What is wrong with you, Darlene? Talk to me."

Darlene grabbed the book from the cushion and slid it onto her lap. She opened the book to page 33 and began reading in a calm, monotone voice.

Having been a superstitious couple, the Ungers rarely traveled into town except to gather necessities. They were content in their reclusive lifestyle, staying far from the clatter and bustle of the rapidly growing community. They never attended church or town meetings. They never attended the annual Christmas tree lighting ceremony on the green. They didn't eat out. They didn't go to shows. They didn't ever travel to the post office to mail packages or to the bank to do their banking, choosing instead to keep their money locked safe-

ly away on the premises. Their only interactions with the public, other than the trips to the grocery store, were during the Halloween season, when Reaper House would open its doors for its annual tradition that shelved the Ungers' hermitic ways for thirteen nights.

Darlene momentarily stopped reading, and, while in what seemed like a trance-like state, her fingers rapidly flipped through the pages and came to a stop on page 101. Then, she continued.

After George Unger's passing in 2003, Isabelle fell into a several-month-long depression. Though she was now alone, George made sure his wife of thirty-four years was provided for, having taken out a hefty life-insurance policy several years before his untimely death. Unfortunately, most of the three-million-dollar inheritance went largely unspent since Isabelle took her own life six years later.

"Hold on," Jamie interrupted. "That must be it."

Samara looked at her curiously. "What must be it?"

"The reason why this is happening. The men in the masks. They're after the money."

"What? But why now, after all these years?"

"I don't know, but what else could it be?"

No sooner did the words leave Jamie's mouth than Darlene's chest heaved like she was having a seizure. Her face shot upward as her teeth clenched, and the veins protruding from her neck pulsed with each beat of her heart. Then, just as quickly, and before Jamie or Samara could react to their friend's mysterious affliction, Darlene's body relaxed and slumped back to its normal position. She opened her eyes and gazed curiously about the room.

"What the hell is going on here? H-how did I get here?"

Samara and Jamie stared at her wide-eyed, a look of terror in their eyes. Jamie spoke first.

"What do you mean, 'how did you get here?'"

Darlene threw her arms in front of her in confusion. "I mean, what am I doing here? How am I in the study right now?"

"Are you serious?" Samara asked.

"Why are you looking at me like that? Of course, I'm serious."

"Darlene," Jamie began, staring intently at her, "where do you think you should be? What's the last thing you remember?"

"I was in the kitchen with Vickie. We had a little disagreement about..," She hesitated, her eyes darting between Samara and Jamie.

"About what?" Jamie asked.

Darlene's eyes faltered. "Well, uh.., about you."

"About *me*?"

"About the problems you went through. You know, when you were seeing things."

"People," Jamie corrected her. "When I was seeing *people*. My parents and little brother."

Darlene dropped her chin to her chest and nodded. "Yeah. She made some wise-ass comment about you being crazy, and it got me so mad."

"Hey, it's okay," Jamie assured her. "I *was* crazy. That's why I was institutionalized. What else do you remember?"

"I remember opening the pantry cabinet, and then..," She fell silent.

"And then what?" Samara asked.

"I-I don't remember anything else except suddenly being in here, with you guys staring at me like I've lost my mind."

Jamie and Samara looked at each other in stunned disbelief. Samara turned to Darlene.

"So then, you don't remember..."

"Darlene," Jamie cut Samara off before she could share the horrific news. "You really don't have any idea what happened here tonight?"

Darlene flashed a concerned look, shifting her stare between the other two. "What? What happened?"

"You lost a lot of time."

"What do you mean?"

"I think something happened to you. You weren't yourself."

"What are you talking about?"

"There's something about this house. Something.., unnatural. I think something took control of you."

"What? What the fuck are you talking about?"

"I don't know how else to explain it. I told you, there's something in this house. It's made me see things. And I think you've seen things too."

Darlene shook her head like she was trying to shake away a memory. "Wh-what?"

"Upstairs in the bedroom," Jamie persisted. "You saw something on the bed, didn't you?"

"I..," Darlene paused as her hands began to shake.

"It's okay, Darlene. What did you see?"

She looked up from her hands, scanning both Samara's and Jamie's faces for signs of judgment but found none.

"I saw Vickie," Darlene said. "She was dead. Someone had stabbed her."

Jamie and Samara looked at each other in shock.

"What?" Darlene questioned. "What's wrong?" She looked around the room. "And where is everybody, anyway?"

Just then, Pierce's voice cried out, "Jamie! Jamie, where are you?" He stumbled into view outside the study's entryway. He looked ragged, on the verge of collapse, and his shirt sleeve was dripping with blood.

Chapter 27

Pierce fell forward into Jamie's arms. He wrapped his right arm around her for support while his left remained by his side, dangling, the blood from his sleeve dripping onto the floor by her feet. Samara and Darlene stood in alarm, causing the book on Darlene's lap to fall to the floor. Darlene's hands flew up to her mouth, her eyes showing enough fear for both of them.

"Pierce, your arm!" Jamie yelped. "What happened?"

"They tried to get in," he answered while gritting his teeth. "I was stupid. When they stopped struggling with the door, I thought I could surprise them. Maybe scare them a little - make them think twice about coming after us. I quickly opened the door and swung the cleaver at them. It was only for a second. They were ready for me. One of them slashed my arm. I dropped the cleaver, but I managed to get the door shut and locked before they could get in."

"Oh my God!" Darlene shouted. "What the fuck is going on?"

Jamie turned her head to Darlene, "There's a lot you need to catch up on."

Samara went to Darlene and put her arms around her to console her, but also to comfort herself.

"Let me see your arm," Jamie said. She bunched up Pierce's shirt sleeve just above the elbow until the large gash in his arm was exposed. Blood trickled down his forearm, gathering at his fingertips in dangling droplets.

"It's deep," she said, concern showing in her voice. "You're going to need stitches."

"You think?" he said dismissively.

She gave him a contemptuous look.

"Sorry," he offered.

"For now, we've got to stop the bleeding." She carefully rolled his sleeve back down. He winced as the fabric slid across the wound. She stuck her fingers into the ripped opening of the sleeve where the weapon had cut him and yanked, tearing a larger gape. A second forceful tug, and the sleeve ripped clean. Pierce let out a sharp yell as his arm jerked from the motion.

"Sorry," she said.

When Pierce composed himself, he replied with a forced grin, "Now we're even."

Jamie quickly wrapped the torn cloth around the gash in his arm while he clenched his teeth and tried to refrain from squirming from the pain. When she was through, Pierce looked at the other two women, and then around him, confusedly.

"Why are you still here?" He questioned. "Where's Shawn? I told him to get you out of here."

"Shawn?" Jamie questioned. "Shawn didn't come back here. We thought he was with you."

Samara started mumbling while inadvertently squeezing Darlene tighter, "No, no, no, no, no, no, no. They got Shawn!"

Darlene shrugged loose from Samara's embrace. "Will somebody tell me what's going on here?" She shrieked. "You guys are scaring the shit out of me."

Jamie whipped her head around. "There are men after us. I'm sorry you have to learn about it this way, but there's no easy way to say it. They've already killed Vickie and Chuck."

Darlene stumbled back, her eyes thrust open. "What?" She looked at Samara's fearful face and then back to Jamie. She grabbed the back of the wingback chair to catch her bearings. "This is a joke, right? You guys are fucking with me."

Nobody answered verbally, but Samara, with tears reforming in her eyes, solemnly shook her head. Jamie snapped right back to business and turned to Pierce.

"I think I know what they want."

He stared at her with a puzzled look in his eyes. "We already know what they want. They want to fucking terrorize us. To kill us."

"They're here for the money," Jamie stated. "We're just in their way."

"Money?" Pierce questioned.

"I think so," Jamie continued. "Isabelle Unger received three million dollars from her husband's life insurance policy. She kept it here, somewhere in the mansion."

"What? How do you know all this?"

She didn't say anything, only twisted her head to look at the book on the floor in front of the sofa. His eyes followed hers.

"What, the book?" he asked.

"It said the Ungers never went to the bank. They kept all their money here."

"We don't even know who wrote the book," he said with a raised voice. "Or if it's even real. You said yourself that it didn't make sense."

"I know. It's just..,"

"Listen, Jamie." He reached forward and clenched her upper arms. "It doesn't matter. Right now, the only thing that matters is getting out of here. I left the two of them at the back door. If they're still there, we can escape through the front."

"But Shawn," Samara stated.

"What?"

"If he didn't come back..?" Her words tapered off.

Jamie, with terror on her face, picked up where Samara left off. "One of them is in the house! Shit!" She turned her stare to Darlene. "Eight plus three."

Darlene shook her head in confusion. "I-I don't know what that means."

"I know," Jamie replied. "Let's go!"

She grabbed Pierce's wrist and pulled him into the hallway foyer, looking left into the long, extended hallway leading to the kitchen. It was empty, quiet. She looked back through the study's archway at her two friends and waved them on. Samara scuttled forward with Darlene following behind. When they stepped into the hallway, Darlene's eyes immediately darted to the body on the floor in the middle of the foyer, the blanket soaked in red. She lost her breath for a moment as she stumbled back and hugged the door jamb, her eyes glued to the hand sticking out from under the covering.

"What the fuck! What the fuck!" she blathered.

"Samara, grab her," Jamie ordered.

With Pierce and Jamie keeping watch on the vacant hallway, Samara jumped to her friend's side. "You need to calm down," Samara said, rubbing her palm along Darlene's cheek, her fingers snaking through her hair at the back of her neck. "You need to be strong."

"V-Vickie?" Darlene questioned, her lower lip quivering.

Samara nodded remorsefully. She looked diagonally down over her shoulder at Vickie's body and then back at Darlene. "Listen to me. We need to get out of here. Do you hear me?"

Darlene gripped the entryway's mouldings tighter. Samara looked into Darlene's frightened eyes and spoke again, slower, but with more conviction.

"Darlene, we can mourn later, but right now, we need to get out of here. Let go of the wall."

With her eyes still cemented on the covered body, Darlene nodded and reluctantly released her hold on the decorative mouldings.

"Good. Now, come on." Samara grabbed Darlene's hand and led her around the body to join with Jamie and Pierce. Pierce ran to the door and grabbed the knob, while the others watched with bated breath, but as before, it wouldn't budge.

"Shit!" he blurted, pounding his fist on the door's hardwood. "It won't open." He turned in frustration, and his face went flush. Jamie noticed his reaction immediately and turned to see what had caused it. Standing down the hallway, facing them, outside the room where Shawn's body was swallowed by the darkness, stood a masked figure, dressed in baggy, white coveralls, his white-gloved hands clenched in fists. He gazed at them through cold, calculating, uncaring eyes.

Chapter 28

The menacing figure stood motionless, his chest heaving in and out. His white gloves and coveralls were displaying blotches of red. He opened his hands and looked at his palms, then rotated them over to admire the blood staining the knuckles.

"What do you want from us?" Jamie screamed, her own hands in fists. Darlene and Samara huddled behind her. Pierce forced his way past the women until he was in front of Jamie. Though stunted by the crude wrap around his gash, blood still trickled down his arm.

The masked figure extended an arm and pointed at Pierce's covered wound. Pierce looked down at the soaked sleeve and back at the threatening figure.

"Yeah, I'm injured. So what? I'll still kick your ass. Come on, Asshole! Come and get me!"

"Pierce! What are you doing?" Jamie cried.

"He doesn't have a weapon," Pierce answered, continuing to stare at the masked attacker. "I can take him. Isn't that right, fucker?" he directed at the stranger. "What's the matter? Now that you don't have a weapon, you're a chicken shit?"

"Pierce, stop it!" Jamie pleaded.

"Jamie, just stay behind me. Please. I know what I'm doing. So, what's it going to be, you dumb fuck? Are you going to make me come to you?"

Pierce managed one step before the white-clad figure reached around his left side with his right hand and pulled a large chef's knife hung from a loop on his outfit. He held it in front of his chest, halting Pierce in his tracks.

"Shit!" Pierce let out.

Jamie tugged on his shirt. "Pierce, we need to go."

"What's the matter, pansy? Too afraid to fight me like a real man? Why don't you put the knife down, you dickless piece of shit?"

The figure tilted his head slightly like a confused puppy, staring Pierce down with squinted eyes. Then, he flipped the handle in his grip and marched forward.

"Oh, fuck!" Pierce yelled. "Run! Run! Get upstairs and hide."

Jamie bolted for the stairs, followed by Samara, Darlene, and then Pierce behind them. When she got to the top of the stairs, Jamie paused half-way across the open landing to where the hallway divided into two directions. She turned and called for the others to hurry. Samara saw the open door to the bathroom on the right and took the opportunity. She darted inside and slammed the door shut.

"Samara, no!" Jamie called out, stepping toward the bathroom, just as Darlene ran past her and dashed down the right corridor. Pierce made it to the top of the stairs and grabbed Jamie's arm to pull her along. She fought against his grip, calling Samara's name. "Samara! Samara!"

"Jamie, let's go!"

"But Samara..." Her words ended abruptly as she saw the top of the masked man's head appear in the stairwell as he gained on them.

"We've gotta go," Pierce urged, giving her arm a yank.

"I don't know where Darlene is," she said in a panic.

"I saw her go this way," Pierce said, pointing to the right. "I'll find her. You go that way and hide." He pointed down the left hallway. "I'll make noise and draw the fucker this way."

She nodded, her eyes bulging with fear. Pierce let her arm go and scrambled down the right hall, yelling, "Darlene!" Jamie ran to her left and ducked into the bedroom Darlene had chosen as hers. She softly closed the door and locked it, then backed away, pacing along the floor. She could hear Pierce's calls for Darlene getting quieter.

The masked figure tramped up the final two stairs and stopped on the balcony's landing, looking ahead at the hallway going in two directions. He could hear Pierce's screams coming from the right direction. He took a step forward, then stopped. He slowly swiveled his head to the right, toward the bathroom door. He stepped up to it and tried the knob, but it was locked. He turned his ear to the door, listening for any sounds, but heard nothing. With his empty fist, he sharply banged on the door. From inside, he heard soft whimpering. He began pounding on the door with both hands, the butt of the knife creating dents in the wood. Samara began screaming incessantly.

Down the hall, Jamie could hear the pounding and the screaming, gutting her right down to her core. She felt like she was going to vomit as she bent over, holding her stomach. She shook her head angrily, covering her ears, trying to block out the pounding and the screaming, the pounding and the screaming, but it was no use. They were in her head, and she couldn't erase what was happening.

The masked figure rammed his shoulder into the door, causing a piece of jamb to splinter and fly off. He rammed the door a second time, and it busted open, slamming into the wall behind it. Samara let out a blood-curdling scream. She began flailing her arms, trying to keep the killer at bay, but it was no use. He charged at her, ramming her like she was another locked door to open. She flew backward into the shower, her back slamming into the hard tiles, knocking the wind out of her. The killer reached forward and grabbed a handful of hair, pulling her out of the shower area. Samara tried screaming through her labored breaths, but was still reeling from the wall. The killer pulled her head up by the hair so she could look into his cold, unfeeling eyes. Then, in the next heartbeat, he shoved her head sideways into the mirror, shattering the glass into a spider's web. Samara's head snapped backward as he let her go, and she crumpled to the floor, barely conscious. She tried reaching for the vanity, but her arm was too heavy. The masked figure reached forward to grab her again, but before he could, he felt a sudden burning sensation in the back of his shoulder, causing him to scream out in pain.

He stumbled backward out of the bathroom, a large piece of the door jamb sticking out of his upper back. He turned to see Jamie standing behind him, bearing her teeth like a rabid dog, her fists clenched for battle.

"You fucking bitch," The killer seethed.

Jamie lunged forward, adrenaline guiding her actions, but her fierceness was short-lived as the masked man punched her in the side of the head, sending her backward and to the floor. The killer looked at her unmoving body, reached his hand over his shoulder, and tugged the pointed shard of wood from his back. With the immediate threat quelled, he then turned back to finish what he'd started.

Stepping into the bathroom, he pulled a lever on the faucet fixture. The round, metal stopper fell over the drain, plugging the sink. He turned on the water and let the sink fill. Placing the knife on the vanity, he reached down and snagged Samara's hair again with one hand, while the other cupped under her chin. He pulled her to her feet as she tried to hammer against his arms with her fists, but she was too weak. He bent her over the vanity and shoved her face into the gathered water. Her body jerked, and her arms flailed wildly as she fought to free herself of his grip. Water splashed violently over the countertop and onto the floor as the killer continued pressing his weight onto her, keeping her face submerged. Samara's legs kicked, slamming into the vanity cabinets with such force that she broke one of the doors off its hinges. She pressed her palms beside the sink for one final desperate shove, hoping it was enough. Air bubbles shot to the surface as Samara gasped for oxygen but took in only water. Then, her struggling ceased, and her body went limp. The killer released his grip, and Samara slid from the counter, her lifeless body hitting the floor.

He turned his head slowly to look over his shoulder. His work wasn't done. He reached for the knife.

Jamie lay on the floor, just then regaining her wits from the shot she'd taken. She pushed herself up to rest on one elbow, while her other hand rubbed the side of her head. Her vision was slightly blurred, but she could see clearly enough to notice the ominous figure emerging from the bathroom and the devastating carnage he'd left behind him. She dug her shoe into the floor to try to push herself back as he took a step forward.

"Get away from her, you son of a bitch!" Pierce charged at the figure and thrust his outstretched palms into the man's chest. His weight and momentum took the figure off his feet, sending him careening through the air, landing halfway down the staircase, and tumbling down the rest of the way. By the time he reached the bottom, it was over.

Jamie forced herself to her feet, slightly wobbly, and made her way to Pierce's side. She looked down to see blood coloring the masked figure's white suit a deep shade of red, the knife protruding from his stomach. She hunched over and let out a heavy breath.

"Are you all right?" Pierce asked.

"I think so," she replied. "Do you think he's dead?"

Pierce looked down the staircase at the bleeding attacker. "I think so. He's not moving, and there's a lot of blood."

"Good. The fucker!"

She looked to her left into the bathroom. "Oh my God! Samara!"

Then, a crashing sound erupted from downstairs in the direction of the kitchen.

Jamie looked at Pierce with widened eyes, "The back door!"

They both knew what it meant. Their tormentors were through playing games.

Chapter 29

Jamie knelt on the bathroom's hard tile floor beside Samara, sobbing and rubbing her deceased friend's wet hair. Pierce stood over her just outside the door, peering down the stairs at the dead stranger in the white uniform, and keeping an eye out for whoever busted in the back door. His eyes were focused, and his thoughts were on one item of business.

"I think I can get the knife," he said quietly.

Jamie remained silent, heavy tears rolling down her cheeks, trickling over her trembling lips, down her neck, and soaking the collar of her shirt.

"I'm going to do it." He stared intently down the staircase.

Jamie wiped the tears away and looked up at him. "What?"

"The knife," he whispered. "I think I can get it."

"Pierce, no!" Jamie responded.

"It's right there." He pointed down the stairs at the blood-covered, fallen figure in white. "We need it."

"You can't," she argued. "We know someone is down there; what if they see you?"

"I'll be careful. If I see someone coming, I'll run back up here."

"But..."

"We need a weapon, Jamie. I can do it."

She turned her head to look at Samara's lifeless body and wondered how all of this came to be. She was only supposed to go through the house and document each room. She shouldn't have invited her friends. And now, because she did, many of them were dead, and the fault rested on her shoulders. But Darlene and Pierce were still with her, and Brandon was out there somewhere. If they planned to get out of this nightmare alive, she couldn't argue. Pierce was right. They needed a weapon. She turned back to him and, with reluctance, nodded her approval.

Pierce gazed nervously down the staircase and over the handrail to see if anyone was coming. Jamie pushed herself up to her feet and quietly walked past him to the balcony railing overlooking the gaudy chandelier hanging above the open foyer. She leaned her upper body over just enough to see the entrance to the hallway leading to the kitchen.

Pierce leaned his back against the wall opposite the stair railing so he could keep his eyes on the open area in case someone were to come into view. Slowly, he stepped down onto the first step, hoping it wouldn't make a sound. It didn't. He took a second step with the same result. He looked up at Jamie's worried face and exhaled in relief. Knowing he didn't have much time, he pointed down and lipped the words, "I'm going." She quickly took a second look over the balcony to calm her nerves.

As softly as he could, walking on his tiptoes, he descended the remaining stairs without stopping, dividing his focus between the hallway, Jamie, and the dead body. When he reached the bottom, he stood beside the ominous figure, watching for any movement. He kicked the bleeding man's leg to ensure he was dead. When he was satisfied it was safe, he crouched over the bloody corpse and gripped the handle of the knife sticking from the lifeless body's stomach. It was then that he heard the enraged yell.

"What did you do? What the fuck did you do?"

Startled, Pierce stood up, yanking the knife from the body, the blade spraying blood in an arc across the wall. Stepping from the hallway, a second masked figure, holding the cleaver Pierce had dropped, came into view. He paused, staring at Pierce holding a knife and standing over the blood-soaked body.

"You fucker! You killed him!"

Pierce's eyes shot upward. "Jamie, run!" he cried.

The masked figure charged at Pierce, the cleaver chambered over his head, ready to strike. Jamie let out a scream and ran across the open floor to the rear wall, where the hallway extended in each direction. She glanced down the left passage as if she were debating which way to go, when really, there wasn't a choice at all. Darlene had run down the right passage and was still missing.

Jamie ran to her right and pounded on the first door on her left before checking the knob.

"Darlene!" she screamed, wiggling the locked doorknob. "Darlene!" She quickly turned around and grabbed the knob across from the first, continuing to call her friend. "Darlene, where are you?" The knob turned, and she shoved the door in a panic. A blast of cold air hit her like a wall, immediately giving her chills. Across the darkened room, a streak of light from the hallway crashed in diagonally, lighting the partial corner of a dark brown dresser, half of a neatly made bed and headboard, and a closed closet door just beyond the bed.

"Darlene! Are you in here?" Jamie questioned loudly, her breath exiting her mouth as vapor. When she didn't receive a response, she was about to exit when she caught sight of the front half of a black, leather shoe exposed at the far end of the light's beam. Jamie questioned again, "Darlene?" The shoe pulled back out of the light. Jamie stiffened as her eyes widened. She took a step into the room, her arm hair tugging at her skin. "Darlene, it's me. You're safe."

From the darkness, above where Jamie had seen the shoe, a pair of solid white eyes opened. Jamie's heart crashed into her ribs. A woman's voice, hoarse and lingering, whispered from the shadows, "The two have returned. Nobody is safe until I'm through." Without turning, Jamie slowly backed away, swinging her arm to the side, blindly grasping for the knob. Her fingers hit the metal just as a leg stepped into the light. She screamed, grabbed the knob, and slammed the door shut.

She grabbed her chest, feeling it tighten as she gasped for air through labored breaths.

"What the hell?" she whispered to herself, trying to rationalize what she'd seen and heard. "Calm down. It was nothing. It's all in your head. You're not seeing things again. That's all in the past. You're better."

Just then, she heard Pierce cry out a shrill scream. Her brain immediately flashed visions of him lying on the floor, his body twitching as he tried to crawl away from his attacker. Her heart sank. Tears flushed from her eyes. She grabbed her stomach, feeling as though she might throw up.

"Why are you doing this?" she cried out through the tears. "Leave us alone!"

Without wasting any more time or effort on the remaining two doors, Jamie streaked down the corridor to the end, where the hallway split in two directions again.

"Darlene!" she yelled. She hadn't been that far into the mansion before and had no idea which way Darlene might have run off to. "Darlene! Where the fuck are you?"

Fear and adrenaline took hold, quickly drying the last of her tears. She looked left, where the hallway led toward the rear of the house, then to the right toward the front, where a window looked out over the front yard and driveway.

"Shit! Fuck!" she mumbled to herself. "Where are you, Darlene?"

She ran down the right passage toward the window, passing by several framed pictures of black cloth, wondering what scares lurked within each, and which would jump out to get her? As she neared the front wall, she slowed, noticing another right turn before the window ahead of her. She paused at the corner and cautiously leaned her head forward to peek around it, her heart still beating a drum solo in her chest.

Around the corner, there were two doors, both closed. One was straight ahead, about five feet. The other door was very narrow and on the right wall, across from the window.

She stepped up to the window and looked out, hoping for a ledge or section of rooftop below that she could climb onto. Instead, it was a long, straight drop to the ground. Her eyes veered to the three vehicles down below, and then right, following the secluded driveway into the distance, where it curved left around a bend, disappearing out of sight.

"Fuck, fuck!" she whispered, inhaling and exhaling like oxygen was a rare commodity. She turned to her right and looked at the two doors. "Darlene," she stated, less as a yell that time, as if she was beginning to lose hope of ever finding her friend. She realized Darlene could have taken the rear hallway, and that any further yelling was only giving away her location to the white-dressed intruders trying to kill her. She looked at the wider door, the less ominous of the two, and opted to check that one first. As she reached for the knob, she heard scuttling footsteps coming from beyond the narrow door. A vision of her friend, frightened and alone, clung to her thoughts. She had to get to her. She grabbed the knob of the narrow door, twisted it, and pulled it open to reveal a dilapidated staircase, leading up to what appeared to be an attic.

She felt herself swallow heavily as she stared up into the unknown. She heard the footsteps. Her friend was there. She knew it. She was going up.

Chapter 30

Her hand blindly slid across the wall at the bottom of the rickety-looking staircase, searching for a light switch. Her fingertip caught a cracked corner of the outlet cover. The sharp plastic tore into her middle finger, leaving a streak of blood on the face plate. She didn't acknowledge the burning sensation. Fear had her well in its grasp, and adrenaline steered her actions. She flipped the switch, but the darkness above remained. She tried a second time, frantically flipping the lever up and down as if she thought she couldn't possibly have done it right the first time. The light was supposed to turn on. It didn't.

The bulb must be out, she thought. She stared up into the darkened attic space, the only light coming from the open door where she stood, her broken shadow creeping up the stairs.

"Darlene," she let out, barely over her normal decibel. "It's Jamie. You need to come down so we can get out of here."

She listened for a reply, hoping her friend heard her plea.

"Darlene, come on!"

The silence was deafening, increasing Jamie's fear and anxiety. She pulled away from the open doorway, glanced around the corner to ensure she was still alone, then back up the stairs. She didn't want to yell and take the chance of the killer hearing her, but she needed to get to Darlene.

"Shit," she said under her breath. She looked down at the first step and felt a chill run down her spine. She already questioned her sanity, but a second question sprang into her head. If she were to go up, should she shut the door behind her in case one of the masked men were to come? *Maybe*, she thought, *it was good that the light didn't work*. She pulled her phone from her back pocket again to check if it had somehow, miraculously, become operational again. It was no use; still dead. She'd have no light. If she left the door open, she'd have just enough light to make her way to the top without breaking her neck, but they'd know where she was. And in the attic, she'd be trapped in a confined space. Neither was a good option.

"Darlene!" she called again, a little louder than the first time. This time, she heard scampering footsteps in the darkness above. It sounded like it came from the left side of the space. She grimaced and clenched her fist, annoyed, the blood from her cut smudging into her palm. "Damn it!"

With her heart pounding and her nerves shot, she took the first step. The wood bowed under her weight, letting out its stress with an unsettling creak. She quickly looked behind her as if the noise had alerted the men in white. It was a ridiculous notion, she told herself, as her voice had already been louder. She took another step, opting to leave the door open, thinking she'd be back down in a minute, her crooked shadow leading the way into the thick, musty air of the black attic space.

"Darlene," she whispered loudly as she closed in on the top step. "Answer me."

She thought she heard deep breathing, but couldn't be sure if it was her own. She stepped onto the top tread, the dust-covered floor of the attic causing her foot to slip away from her. Her hand managed to grab the railing in time to keep her from falling backwards. She let out a gasp and pulled herself upright. Another gasp, mimicking hers, echoed from the darkness to her left.

"Darlene," Jamie whispered. "It's me. I can't see you. Can you come to me?"

"No," a barely audible whisper replied. "I'm afraid."

"Okay, stay there; I'll come to you."

Jamie cautiously stepped forward out of the downstairs light's reach.

"Where are you?" she questioned.

A faint whisper returned, "I'm here."

The whisper came from a short distance ahead of her. She took another step, and her head hit an exposed roof joist, causing her to reel back and yell in pain.

"Ow! Fuck!" She squeezed her palm against her forehead and felt a lump had already formed. Determined to find her friend, she ducked her head and took another step forward, waving her arms in front of her to prevent another accident. Shuffling forward a few more inches, her hand felt something dangling from the ceiling. For a brief moment, she lost touch with it until it swung back against the back of her wrist. She spun her hand around and snatched it. She knew immediately what it was: a string hanging from a ceiling light fixture. She gently tugged on the line, praying for a working bulb. The light flashed on, blinding her, as she first closed her eyes and then slowly opened them to a squint. Looking through her eyelashes, she saw only a blur in front of her. Slowly, her vision began to clear as the large attic opened up ahead of her.

She thought she'd find Darlene, crouched on the floor in front of her, hugging her knees in fear, anxiously waiting to be rescued. Instead, the room was mostly empty, with only a few pieces of moldy furniture shoved to one side, and a large, creepy-looking clown statue propped in the corner. Its smile was inviting in a John Wayne Gacy sort of way.

On the wall beside the clown, there was another door cracked open a sliver. Above the door was a sign, its words painted to look like running blood, dripping from the ceiling.

Hall of Tortured Souls. Nice, she thought sarcastically. *Just what I need right now.* "Darlene?" she said in her normal voice. "Say something so I know where you are." Her eyes shifted left and right as she slowly strolled forward, looking around the furniture in case her friend was curled up in a ball, hiding. She continued forward, her gaze landing on the smiling clown. She curled her lip in disgust. Then, her focus shifted to the cracked door, a hint of darkness showing beyond it from the opening. Suddenly, a wave of frigid air surrounded her, and goosebumps formed on her arms. She felt herself shiver. She wrapped her arms tightly around her chest, her bloody finger staining her upper sleeve with red. She let out a breath that plumed in front of her, and her lips quivered.

"Jesus Christ, it's cold up here," she said, mostly to herself, but if her friend heard her, all the better.

She stepped to the door and tried to peek into the opening, but it was too dark. "Are you in there?" Jamie questioned.

"I'm here," came a reply, but it was from behind her.

Startled, Jamie spun around. When she glimpsed the sight, she clasped her hand over her mouth to prevent her scream from echoing downstairs, and threw herself backwards against the door, slamming it shut. Her eyes bulged out of her head, and her muscles tightened.

Standing before her, staring through blank eyes, was a child - a boy - maybe in his early teens. He wore clothes that were in tatters and stained with blood. His hair was dark brown, his skin pasty white. Lacerations decorated his flesh along his arms, neck, and cheeks. Jamie could see large, gaping wounds on his chest and stomach through the torn fabric of his clothes. The knees of his pants were covered in dirt and grass stains. His face showed no emotion as he stared into Jamie's panic-stricken eyes. Jamie, on the other hand, was a heartbeat away from a full-blown panic attack.

She forced her eyes shut, her nose releasing mucus that spilled onto her quaking hand. *It has to be in my head. That's it. The fear has gotten to me. I must be hallucinating. I can just will it away.* With that thought, she swallowed heavily and slowly opened her eyes, shaking from both the cold and the fear. Her shoulders loosened and dropped. She let out a relieved gasp when she saw she was faced with an empty room. But before she could catch her bearings, she felt a cold breath whisp across the right side of her neck, and the pungent smell of death invaded her nose. She slowly, hesitantly turned her head to her right.

"WHAT DID YOU DO TO MY BROTHER?" The deathly-looking boy shrieked.

Jamie screamed, throwing her body backward into the large clown. The statue hit the wall hard and rocked on its base before tipping forward. She caught its trajectory out of the corner of her eye and dove out of the way, slamming her shoulder into an olive-green recliner as she hit the floor. The clown smashed into the floor between her and the boy with a loud thud.

Jamie whipped her chin over her shoulder to see the boy standing by the door to the Hall of Tortured Souls, the statue creating a barrier between them. Without hesitation, she dug the toes of her shoes into the floor and pushed off like a sprinter at the start of a race. She ran for the stairwell, narrowly avoiding slipping on the dusty floor until she made it to the top of the stairs, where her right foot skidded out from underneath her as she stepped onto the top tread. She fell backward, her lower back slamming against the front of the top stair tread. She yelped in pain as her body slid down the stairs, her shoulder blades getting chewed up by the rough wood. Her foot caught the edge of the lower door frame, slowing her descent, before she spilled out into the hallway in front of the window.

She kicked her leg out and shoved the door closed with her shoe before whoever, *whatever* that thing was, could come for her. She grabbed her lower back and winced, forcing herself onto her knees, and then her feet. She had no idea what she had just encountered, if anything, but she wasn't sticking around to find out. She lunged for the corner to head back in the direction from which she came. When she darted around the wall, it was like she collided into an immovable object, smacking headfirst into a man's brawny chest.

Chapter 31

"Gotcha!" The voice said as arms wrapped around her.

Jamie screamed in sheer horror as she squirmed to break free from his grasp.

"Whoa! Calm down! Jamie, it's me."

Jamie stopped her struggling just long enough to recognize that it was Pierce holding her, his face a refreshing sight, yet his eyes fearful.

"Oh my God, Pierce!" she cried out. She excitedly slammed herself into him and squeezed him in the tightest hug she could. "I thought you were dead."

He held her tight, his cheek resting on the top of her head. "I'm right here. I've been looking for you. Where were you?"

She pulled away, pointing around the corner as she spoke. "I thought I heard Darlene up in the..," Then, her eyes registered Pierce's appearance. "Oh my God! Your face."

His left eye was bruised and swollen, as was his cheek below it, and his lower lip was split open where it looked like a tooth had punctured it.

"I'm all right," he answered, playing it off. "But we've gotta go."

"But..."

"Now, Jamie!"

He grabbed her by the wrist and yanked her forward down the corridor to where the hallway split. As he turned down the left passage in the direction of the open balcony landing, Jamie's eyes woefully glanced behind her.

"What about Darlene?" she cried.

"I can't worry about her right now," he answered. "I've gotta get you outta here. We can send help."

Jamie strained a little in his grasp, struggling with the idea of leaving her best friend, but she knew he was right. They didn't know where Darlene was, and their opportunities for escape were limited and quickly dwindling. She stopped resisting and followed his lead. She wanted out of the house.

They turned the second corner onto the open balcony at the top of the main staircase. As they neared the top step, Jamie slowed her pace and looked into the bathroom. Samara's distorted, wet frame lay lifeless on the tile floor. Jamie stiffened and froze, slipping free from Pierce's grip, halting him at the top of the stairs. He looked back at her.

"Jamie, let's go!"

She turned her head to look at him, and as he spoke, his words came out slow and heavy, like he was talking to her through a pane of glass.

"She's dead," he yelled. "You can't help her."

Suddenly, every muscle in Jamie's body became rigid. Her face shot upward as her teeth clenched and her neck tightened, displaying protruding veins. Her arms extended downward, her hands thrust open with her fingers splayed. Her legs tensed, and her body rose onto her toes like she was a ballerina. In the next heartbeat, her eyes fluttered wildly as visions flashed in her head, and she was instantly displaced to her right, three feet from where she stood.

She was calm but confused as she stared at a woman at the top of the stairs, where she, herself, had stood seconds before. The bathroom door was closed and in one piece, and Pierce was no longer in sight. The woman, maybe in her early thirties, had auburn hair pulled tightly into a bun at the back of her head. She wore a tight red, long-sleeved shirt with an open, white cardigan sweater over her shoulders, a red, patterned plaid skirt, and dark stockings. Her eyes were wide, and her cheeks were flushed as she stood frozen at the top of the staircase. In the next moment, an older woman sprang from around the corner where Jamie and Pierce had just run from. Jamie was helpless to step in as it all happened so quickly. In a flash, the elderly woman latched onto the young woman's head and twisted violently. Jamie heard the snapping sound as the woman crumpled to the floor in a heap. Seeing what had just happened, she instinctively extended her hand and screamed out, but no sound came from her mouth. Still, the older woman stopped, turned her head toward Jamie as if she had heard something, flashed a devious grin, and then bent over to grab the dead woman.

The murderer's name came to Jamie in an instant. *Isabelle Unger.*

Gripping the ankles, Isabelle slid the woman across the floor, directly toward Jamie. Jamie didn't have time to react, but it didn't matter; Isabelle and the woman she'd just killed passed through her as if she were a ghost, which was ridiculous, because Jamie didn't believe in ghosts. Not anymore.

She patted herself down to ensure she was still solid and whole, and then turned to watch Isabelle drop the woman's legs in front of the wall across from the bathroom. Isabelle bent over, pressed the head of a screw at the center of an outlet cover, and a panel in the wainscoting clicked and slid open, revealing a hidden space. She watched as Isabelle dragged the young woman's body into the confined cubby, exited the space, and pressed the screw in the outlet cover again, sealing the wall as if nothing had happened.

Isabelle turned and looked into Jamie's eyes. She brought her index finger to her lips.

"Shhhh."

Then, Jamie heard the panicked scream.

"Jamie! What's wrong?"

Her body immediately relaxed, returning to its normal state, where she stood, once again, at the foot of the bathroom. Pierce latched onto her arm.

"Are you okay?"

Confused, Jamie reacted to his question without thinking.

"Yes. Yeah."

"Then, let's go." He nodded his head sideways down the stairs.

She had no idea what had just happened, but she knew what she had just witnessed. Somehow, she was transported to that Halloween night in 2009 when Isabelle Unger killed those people. She watched in horror as Isabelle stuffed that woman's body in a hidden room.

"Come on!" Pierce urged, squeezing her wrist.

She nodded, still in shock from the sudden vision she'd encountered. She knew it was somehow real and not just an unexplainable hallucination. Her terrified eyes glanced to her right at the solid wall, where the ridges in the wainscoting concealed a horrifying secret.

Chapter 32

Jamie felt her breathing shallow as they approached the bottom of the staircase. Pierce held her hand on the way down, making sure they stayed together. Her head shot sideways over the railing to get a glimpse down the hallway leading to the kitchen in case another masked figure appeared.

'Eight plus three' sprang to the forefront of her thoughts.

Pierce slowed his pace as they rounded the banister's decorative newel post. He stepped over the leg of the masked man he'd shoved down the stairs. Jamie stepped between the masked man's legs and glanced to her left into the library. She froze, yanking Pierce back.

"What?" he asked, looking back.

She pointed into the library. "The knife."

Sitting on the floor with his upper body propped against the front wall, the second masked figure lay motionless, the chef's knife impaled in his chest. His white suit showed blotches of blood seeping around holes in the fabric where he'd been stabbed several times during the men's struggle.

"Right," Pierce said, stepping back over the first figure. "Good thinking."

He released Jamie and quickly stepped to the seated dead man. She turned her head away as Pierce reached for the knife's handle. Seeing the knife sticking out of a person was one thing. Seeing it yanked out was something completely different. Turning her head only served to remind her of the amount of death she'd seen that day, as Vickie's body lay a few feet from her under the red-stained blanket. From behind her, she heard a faint liquidy sound as Pierce pulled the knife free from the attacker's chest. Her eyes narrowed, and she brought her left fist to her mouth as she swallowed, the sound of the exiting knife making her feel slightly queasy.

"Okay, let's go," Pierce said, rubbing his hand under her bent elbow as he passed by.

He cautiously led the way down the hallway toward the kitchen, the bloody knife in his hand extended forward. Jamie stayed close, her left hand wrapped around his right bicep. As they neared the back of the staircase, Jamie noticed wet drops of blood on the hardwood floor. She looked at Pierce's wrapped arm inquisitively.

"Are you bleeding?"

He turned his head slightly but continued to look forward. "What?"

"Your arm. Is it still bleeding?"

He glanced at the makeshift sleeve bandage wrapped around his wounded arm. "No, I don't think so."

"Then, what's this blood from?"

Pierce turned his head to her with concern in his eyes. Jamie pointed to the floor. He looked down and saw the drops of blood she'd pointed out. His eyes quickly followed the trail in front of them, leading into the bedroom behind the staircase.

"It's going into the bedroom," he replied. "Stay behind me."

Jamie squeezed his arm tighter. Pierce slowly made his way toward the bedroom's doorway, the blood disappearing into the darkness. He extended his right hand holding the knife into the open doorway while his left hand reached across his body to feel for a light switch along the inside of the wall. His fingers first brushed across some exposed wires from a missing switchplate before rubbing over the top of the switch and toggling it to the on position.

"Oh, shit!" Pierce let out, stumbling backward from the sight.

Jamie couldn't help herself. She peeked around the door jamb to see what had him startled. She immediately regretted that decision.

Shawn was lying in a pool of his own blood, his mouth wide open, and his eyes bulging from their sockets. His neck had been split open like a ravine, where barbed wire had been pulled so tight that it nearly ripped his head from his shoulders. His hands were near the gaping wound, bloody and chewed up, where he wrestled hopelessly to free himself from the barbs.

Jamie turned away, covering her mouth and bending over, hoping she could keep down the contents of her stomach.

"Fuck!" Pierce yelled. "We've gotta keep going."

Jamie held back tears, closing her eyes tightly and slowly trying to catch her breath.

"Jamie, look at me," Pierce said sternly.

Jamie's bloodshot eyes fluttered open to look at him.

"You can do this," he said in a calmer voice. "You're going to get out of here. I'm going to get you out of here. But we have to keep going."

Jamie pursed her lips and nodded. She stood up, holding her stomach, and grabbed Pierce's arm again. They continued forward, reaching the kitchen, where Pierce pointed across the room to the back hallway.

"The back door," he said. "That's where they came in. That's where we're going out."

"Are you sure it's safe?" Jamie questioned.

"I don't know, but we have to try."

He trodded across the kitchen with Jamie in tow, keeping his eyes alert. Jamie stared nervously over his shoulder as they rounded the corner into the rear hall.

The back door was busted in, as Pierce suspected, the upper half cocked at an angle, pulled from its hinges. He turned his head to Jamie.

"Be careful."

"You too."

They slid forward, alert and cautious, stepping over broken fragments of wood. Pierce eased the crippled door aside and leaned his head out of the doorway. The overhead floodlight cast its beam partially over the cemetery, the gravestones, half in light and half in shadow, marking the path to freedom.

"It's clear," Pierce said. "Let's go."

He stepped out onto the small concrete patio, keeping his eyes peeled for movement. Jamie stepped out behind him, putting her hand on his shoulder for support and signaling him to lead her away from the god-awful mansion. He complied by stepping forward onto the pathway that led to the side of the house. They had gotten maybe ten feet before Pierce stopped, frozen in his tracks. At his feet, a severed hand lay on the grass just beside the path. Jamie heard him take in a deep breath and dropped her eyes to the ground. She saw the hand and quickly averted her eyes to her left. When she did, she audibly gasped, covering her mouth to keep from making too much noise. In that moment, she felt her blood drain from her face, and she lost feeling in her body. If she hadn't been holding onto Pierce's shoulder, she would have found herself hitting the ground.

Draped over a gravestone, Chuck's lifeless body clung to the rough top surface of the granite. His right arm was missing below the shoulder, as was his left leg from the knee down. The back of his shirt was sliced to pieces, with chunks of flesh sprouting through the openings. Blood had trickled from his body, streaking down the face of the headstone, coloring the inscribed letters with red. It was then that Jamie saw it.

"Oh my God!" she blurted.

"Don't look at him," Pierce responded, trying to remain strong.

Jamie grabbed Pierce's shirt sleeve, bunching it in her shaking fist. When he felt her grip, he looked at her and saw the fear in her eyes. She pointed.

"No, that," she replied.

He followed her finger to where Chuck lay in tatters over the gravestone. Just below the body, on the headstone's face, he saw what had captured her attention.

"What the hell?" he let out.

It was something that couldn't be, yet there it was, an undeniable, unexplainable mystery.

"How is that even possible?" Pierce asked.

"I-I don't know," Jamie replied.

There, carved into the granite headstone:

Charles Sebastian Weaver
Born 1998, Died 2025.

Chapter 33

They both stared at the gravestone, petrified. Neither thought they would be fortunate enough to escape the horror of seeing their dead friend, but what they beheld was beyond anything they could have imagined, especially seeing his name carved into the very headstone he lay across.

"H-how..?" Jamie stumbled for the words.

"I don't know," Pierce answered, shaking his head. "We don't have time to figure out all the weird shit that's going on here. Come on." He urged her onward.

He managed a single step before Jamie grabbed the back of his shirt, stopping him.

"Pierce!" she alerted him in an anxious, high-pitched voice.

"What is it?"

"There," she replied, pointing to another head-stone just past where Chuck's was.

Here lies Richard Andrew DeStello
Born 1999, Died 2025.

"That's Vickie," Jamie said, confused. "What the hell is going on here?" She swung her body around to look at the stones on the other side of the narrow path. "Another one," she said, tapping Pierce on the wrist with one hand while pointing with the other. He turned curiously.

Shawn Stephen Higgins
December 1997-September 2025.

"There's one, too," Pierce added, pointing diagonally ahead of them.

Samara Marie Ludendorff
Born 1999, Died 2025.

"It's *us*," Jamie said, shaken, her voice exiting through quivering lips. "It's all of us."

"No, it's not," Pierce answered. "I don't know what the fuck this is, or what kind of game someone is playing, but *we're* still alive. And I plan on keeping it that way. We've gotta keep moving."

Without another word, Pierce grabbed Jamie's wrist and tugged her forcefully, striding quickly along the path. They neared the side of the house when Jamie froze again.

"No, no, no, no," she let out. "Fuck!"

Pierce stopped and glanced to his left, becoming rigid, his face losing all color.

"Why is this happening?" Jamie cried. She stared at another stone, this one carved with an unexpected name.

Brandon Drew Landon
Born 1999, Died 2025.

"They must have gotten him on the road," she said. "Why are they doing this?"

She didn't receive an answer, as Pierce suddenly seemed oblivious to her presence. She looked up at him and noticed his nervous stare. His gaze wasn't on Brandon's headstone but on two others.

"Pierce!" Jamie spoke loudly, snapping him from his trance-like state.

"Y-yeah?" he questioned, looking at her with his eyes bugged out.

"I think Brandon's dead, too." She nodded her chin toward the grave she stood before.

Pierce glanced at it, let out a defeated breath, then turned his head away. "Let's go."

He trodded forward, determined. As Jamie followed, she noticed him peek back over his left shoulder at the two markers he seemed entranced by. She quickly looked while keeping pace with him, but she nearly stumbled when she saw the names. Her thoughts scattered in all directions. Goosebumps trailed up and down her arms. Her breath left her for a moment before she had no choice but to let it out in a labored huff.

She quickly ran to Pierce's side as they turned the corner at the rear of the house and hustled along the side of the building.

"D-did you see that?" She questioned, keeping her stride with his.

"See what?" He kept his focus forward, keeping a watchful eye.

"The names. On the graves."

"Yes. Our friends are dead. I know," Pierce responded, distressed.

"No," Jamie said as they made it to the front of the house and stepped into the driveway. "The other two. The boys."

"What boys?"

"Oh, right." She shook her head in confusion. "I didn't tell you."

"Tell me what?"

"There were two boys who died here a few years ago. Brothers. Thomas and Rory Wilkinson."

"Yeah, so?"

"Their graves were there, too. Didn't you see them? You were staring right at them."

"I don't know; I wasn't paying attention. Jesus, Jamie, why all the questions? What do I care about two kids that died here a few years ago? I'm trying to get us out of here before our names end up on a couple of gravestones like the rest of our friends." He hurried down the driveway with Jamie shuffling behind him, trying to keep up.

"But their headstones," she continued. "The engraving had their birth years, but it didn't list when they died."

"So what? What is that supposed to mean?"

"I don't...maybe they aren't dead...and...I don't know." *'The two had returned,'* jumped into her head.

"I don't know either, so can we forget about all that and concentrate on getting out of here?"

Jamie furrowed her brow. "Y-yeah."

They hurriedly continued around the bend in the driveway, where the land dipped down toward its long descent to the main road. Up ahead, the large tree lay across the driveway; on either side, the land sloped down and dropped off a steep ledge, making it nearly impossible to go around.

They approached the tree, the moonlight guiding their way. Pierce gripped the knife he held tightly in his hand, ready for anything. Jamie leaned over the large tree trunk to see how sharply the driveway dipped.

"Be careful," Pierce said. "Let me help you over."

He grabbed Jamie's left hand as she kicked her right leg over the fallen tree. He held her tight while she gathered her footing on the sloped, gravelly surface. Once balanced, she swung her left leg over, catching her pant leg on a limb and tearing a small rip in the fabric.

"Shit!"

"You okay?" Pierced asked.

"Yeah. Just a small scratch on my ankle."

"Okay, help me over," Pierce said.

"Wait!" Jamie said, throwing her chin skyward, her eyes rolling to one corner of her lids.

"What?"

"Shhh. Do you hear that?"

"What?" Pierce asked again.

Jamie put her hand up to silence him as she slowly made her way to the side of the driveway, letting her ear follow the sound.

"It sounds like ringing?" Jamie said, easing herself to the drop-off at the edge of the driveway. She cautiously leaned forward and stared down a twenty-foot drop to a rock formation at the base of the ridge. Her eyes first caught the glow of a lit cellphone screen. Excitedly, she yelled, "It's a phone! It's a..." Her words went silent. Her jaw hung open as her eyes caught sight of the rear tire of a motorized scooter. To the left of it, the broken, distorted body of Brandon, his head wrenched unnaturally about his shoulders. "Oh my God!"

"Jamie," Pierce stated.

"It's Brandon," she said, covering her mouth.

"Jamie," Pierce repeated, more urgently.

"He must have fallen off the side."

"Jamie!" Pierce screamed, getting her attention.

She turned to see a look of dread on his face as he stared past her. She rotated to see a white-masked figure, like the others, charging up the driveway. The moon's light glinted off a machete in his hand as his pace increased purposefully, his gaze locked on Jamie.

"Come on, come on!" Pierce yelled, holding out his left hand.

Jamie sprinted back to the center of the driveway and lunged for Pierce's hand. He latched onto her, planting one foot up onto the tree for support as he pulled. She managed one bent knee onto the top of the large oak as Pierce yanked her upper body, causing her to fall forward over the tree, landing on her chest on the hard, unpaved surface.

The menacing figure in white continued forward, gaining ground.

"Are you all right?" Pierce asked, helping Jamie to her feet, all the while keeping his eyes glued on the oncoming attacker.

"Yeah," she said, winded from the landing. "I'll live."

"Not if we don't get out of here now," Pierce yelled. "Go! Back to the house!"

"What about you?" she cried.

"I'll be right behind you. Just go!"

Her eyes shifted to the man in white, then to Pierce, then up the driveway. Without another word, she ran, hoping Pierce was close behind.

Chapter 34

Instinctively, Jamie darted for the front porch; it was the closest entrance to the house. Her mind was in a panic, and terror directed her actions. She launched herself up the stairs, skipping the first and third, and nearly crashed into the door from her momentum. It was only when she reached for the knob that she recalled how the door wouldn't previously open. In a frenzy, she gave it an adrenaline-fueled twist anyway, and the door popped open. She shoved it with her shoulder and barged in, tripping on the first dead attacker's arm. She dropped to the floor, smashing her knee into the hardwood, her head coming within inches of her friend Vickie's covered face. She froze for a moment, ignoring the burning sensation she felt in her leg, while images of her own death at the hands of a crazed, machete-wielding killer flashed before her. That thought alone was enough to motivate her to her feet.

Pressing her palms to the floor, she pushed herself up onto one leg. Searing pain shot through her knee, and her leg gave out. She tried to catch herself but stumbled backward toward the foyer's staircase and fell on her butt with her back crashing against the newel post. From the impact, her head jerked backward and hit the corner edge of the post, making an awful cracking sound. She didn't need to feel her head to know she'd been cut open; the sensation of blood trickling down the back of her scalp was enough. She reached behind her and squeezed her palm to her head, clenching her teeth in pain. Her chin shot up, and her vision blurred as she tried to focus on the large chandelier hanging from the beam in the second floor's vaulted ceiling.

And then, in an instant, the pain was gone, and she was no longer sitting on the floor.

She stood in the center of the foyer, looking at the floor around her, the two dead bodies absent from sight. She turned her head to see that the door behind her was now closed. Everything was quiet, calm. She didn't feel that overwhelming sense of dread she had felt seconds before. She was confused about how she got there, but remembered hitting her head and feeling wetness in her hair. She reached for the back of her skull, and when she did, her head leaned back slightly, just enough for her eyes to catch the bottom of the boy's sneakers.

The shocking sight caused her to stagger back as her eyes took in the entire scene. Thirteen-year-old Rory Wilkinson dangled from the massive light fixture, his body limp and motionless. His face and hands were pale white, the skin on his cheeks showing signs of decomposition. Jamie felt herself taking in a deep breath, the chilled air burning her lungs. Before she could turn away, the boy's leg twitched. Her eyes expanded, filled with fear, as she watched the boy's body begin to convulse violently. She backed away, fearing the chandelier would rip clean from the support beam and come crashing down upon her. As her back pressed against the front door, Rory's spasms suddenly ceased. She stood in shock, staring up at the swaying boy, bringing her hand to her chest to keep her heart from exploding through her ribs. She exhaled heavily, watching her breath float in the air in front of her. Then, she looked on in horror as the boy's eyes snapped open. Her arms became numb as she watched his head swivel to face her. His chapped, pale lips opened, and he spoke.

"The reaper has been summoned. The two have returned."

Jamie gasped, and in the next moment, she found herself once again sitting at the base of the staircase, her back against the newel post. Rory Wilkinson was gone, her friend and the masked stranger back in the foyer, lying in pools of their own blood.

She pulled her hand from the back of her head and trembled at the sight of the crimson liquid smeared across her palm. Just then, Pierce feverishly ran through the open front door. He saw Jamie sitting on the floor, her face flushed, and he slammed the door shut.

"He's coming!" Pierce yelled fearfully. He locked the deadbolt and pressed his butt to the door. Out of breath, he bent over and supported himself with his hands on his knees.

Jamie looked at him from her position on the floor and mumbled something. Breathing heavily, he looked at her, confused.

"What?"

"The two have returned," she repeated under her breath.

"What are you talking about?" Pierce questioned.

"The boys," she replied. "Thomas and Rory Wilkinson. It must be them."

"What must be them?"

"The ones who are after us. They've returned."

"You said they were killed. You saw their graves out back. People don't come back from the dead."

Jamie's eyes shifted around the foyer. "It's this house. There's something about it. Strange things keep happening, and..." She paused, narrowing her eyes like something had just come to her. "Wait, what did you say just now?"

"I said, people don't come back from the dead."

"You said they were killed," Jamie responded. "I told you two boys died here. I never said they'd been killed."

"Well, I...I just assumed after what we've been dealing with."

Jamie shook her head to clear her thoughts. "I think somehow they've come back."

"Enough with this stuff, Jamie. There's someone out there trying to kill us. We need to come up with a plan. We need to get out of here."

"It's one of them," she said, glancing up at the chandelier. "I saw him. He spoke to me. Isabelle Unger, too."

"Jesus Christ, Jamie! I thought we were done with this shit. The hospital was supposed to fix you. Now it's happening all over again. You're acting crazy, talking about seeing ghosts."

"I'm not crazy!" Jamie yelled. "Don't call me crazy!"

Pierce stood from the door, putting his hands up in front of his chest to calm Jamie down, his right hand clutching the knife, his left arm bleeding from the wound he'd sustained earlier.

"I'm sorry," he said. "I didn't mean it like that. I'm just really stressed right now. Our friends are dead, and there's a guy out there coming after us, and I'm trying to keep you safe."

Jamie tilted her head like a confused puppy as she stared at the blood trickling down his injured left arm.

"I'm scared that I won't be able to save you," Pierce's voice rose as he continued, "and you're sitting there talking about hearing dead kids and some crazy woman who killed herself sixteen years ago."

Jamie pushed her feet into the floor and slid her back up the bottom post, still focused on Pierce's arm.

"You're right-handed," she mumbled.

Pierce threw his arms outward in confusion. "What the hell, Jamie? Yes, I'm right-handed. You know that. What does that have to do with me getting you out of here?"

"Earlier, when you said one of them attacked you," she pointed to the dead masked man on the floor to his right, "you told us you swung the cleaver at them, and they cut you, causing you to drop the weapon."

"Yeah. That's what happened."

"How would they have cut your left arm? Wouldn't you have been holding the cleaver in your right hand – swinging at them with your right?"

"I..," he stumbled with his words. "I don't remember. I must have had it in my left hand at that time. A lot was going on."

"And Brandon?" she questioned, her eyes wide.

"What about him?" Pierce asked.

"You said you watched him ride off down the driveway after you helped him get his scooter over the tree. How did he end up at the bottom of that ridge right where the tree was?"

"Is this really what we're doing? We don't have time to..,"

"Make the time," Jamie said sternly. "How did Brandon end up at the bottom of that ridge?"

Pierce shook his head, his lower jaw ticking up and down like he wanted to say something but was unsure.

"He...he must have come back," Pierce said unconfidently.

"You're lying," Jamie said nervously, staring into his eyes. "Please tell me you didn't."

"What?" Pierce said, aggravated.

"You didn't watch Brandon ride down the driveway at all, did you?"

"Jamie, you need to stop. You're talking crazy. I'm trying to get you out of here."

"You never helped him over the tree."

"Jamie." Pierce looked at her disappointedly.

"You pushed him, didn't you?"

Everything went silent for a moment as Pierce dropped his chin to his chest. When he looked back up, something had changed in his eyes. He was no longer the Pierce Jamie knew. Then, from behind him, a pounding on the front door caused him to jump, and suddenly, he was back to himself.

"Fuck! He's here!" Pierce screamed, turning toward the door and pressing his palms to it. "Run, Jamie! Get out of here. Go hide!"

Jamie squeezed her knee, shook her leg a few times to extinguish the pain, then hobbled up the staircase toward the second floor, the entire time terrified that what she had been thinking could be true.

Chapter 35

Jamie scrambled up three-quarters of the staircase, hearing the loud banging on the front door below, before she had to give her injured leg a rest. She fell to her palms and crawled the rest of the way, one tread at a time, leaving smudges of blood from her hand on a few steps. Over her shoulder, she could hear Pierce screaming.

"You're not taking her! Do you hear me? Let her go!"

Jamie heaved herself up the last step onto the balcony, breathing heavily. She hadn't overexerted herself, but the fear had gripped her, and her chest had tightened to the point where she couldn't breathe. She looked to her right into the open bathroom, where Samara's cold, blank stare accosted her.

She grabbed hold of the balcony railing and pulled herself to her feet, ignoring the pain in her head and leg. With the railing offering her support, she looked down at the carnage on the first floor. Vickie was dead. One of the masked attackers was dead. From her vantage point, she could just see into the library, where another attacker was dead, his legs barely in view. There was a third masked person outside the door (*eight plus three*, she thought), threatening to get in. And Pierce, with his back to her, holding back the bad man from kicking the door in.

"Pierce!" she cried.

"Go! Hide!" he yelled back without turning away from his struggle to keep the door intact.

Her shoulders tensed, and she looked behind her at the hallways leading in opposite directions. The left hallway was easier to traverse, but limited in its locations to hide, having only four bedrooms. She'd be trapped, with no way of escape. The right hallway had more places to hide, but as she rubbed her stained palm down her thigh to her knee and felt a sharp pain streak up to her hip, she didn't think she'd make it far.

"Fuck, fuck, fuck!" she whispered to herself before turning her head to her left, where the image of Isabelle Unger dragging a woman into a hidden cubby flashed into her head. *The secret room*, she thought.

Her eyes veered downward near the bottom of the wall, where an inconspicuous outlet cover possibly held the key to her survival.

She hobbled forward, glancing down through the balusters to see that Pierce was still distracted from the stranger's constant banging. She leaned down, reaching for what looked like a screwhead in the center of the outlet cover, all the while thinking she must be out of her mind to believe that her earlier vision was real. She knew nothing would happen when she pressed the screw. Only, something did.

Before her eyes, a panel in the wainscoting shifted and slid open, revealing a darkened crawl-space in the wall. At first, she was nervous to crawl inside, thinking she might get trapped in there once the door closed. Then, she decided the Ungers wouldn't have built a secret room in the wall without having a means of getting out.

The banging from the first floor suddenly ceased. Jamie didn't know what it meant, but her mind automatically jumped to the conclusion that it couldn't be good. She peered into the darkness of the cubby, took in a deep breath, and crawled inside.

Her hands slid along some fabric on the floor as she contorted herself to squeeze into the tiny space. She frantically felt along the interior walls, searching for another button or lever with which to close the panel. There had to be something. In seconds, she found what she was looking for, a small round button the size of a doorbell affixed to the wall just inside the sliding door. She pressed the button, but before the panel door slid back into place, she heard the man on the other side of the door bellow the words that caused her heart to drop.

"Open the fucking door, Pierce!"

Chapter 36

Jamie held back tears in the dark out of fear that the floodgates would open. Her soul felt much like her current situation: pitch black. Her mind was racing. She knew what she heard; it was unmistakable. The masked stranger outside called Pierce by his name. They knew each other. But how? Why? It seemed like Pierce was doing everything he could to protect her.

She wasn't thinking clearly, she told herself. After all, she had yelled Pierce's name several times. Hell, the man must've known *her* name by now, too. Still, there were other signs. Like Pierce's injury, and the way he acted when she questioned him about Brandon. He wasn't himself.

Her thoughts shifted to Darlene, who was still missing somewhere in the house. *She* hadn't been acting herself, either. It was like someone, or some*thing*, had possessed her for a while. Had the same happened to Pierce? Even Jamie herself had shown signs of unusual behavior, and strange occurrences had been happening around her. That's how she ended up in the tiny crawlspace, after all. If it hadn't been shown to her by Isabelle Unger, she wouldn't have known about the secret cubby.

Whatever was going on, for now, she felt safe. She sat on the floor with her legs extended in front of her and let her shoulders relax, but they couldn't relax enough. The back of her head was on fire from the gash she sustained. When she brought her hand up to feel how bad the wound was, her arm grazed against a string dangling from above. She knew instantly what it was. She waved her hand aimlessly in the dark in front of her face until she had the string in her fingers. She gave it a light tug, and a bulb on the ceiling above the door panel illuminated.

At first, she closed her eyes and turned away, the light blinding her. Then, she slowly opened her eyes - only a crack - to let her pupils acclimate to the brightness. Once they had adjusted, she turned her head back to face forward, only to be horrified by the sight.

She threw her hand to her mouth to keep from screaming and crashed into the wall on her right as she tried shimmying sideways in the cramped space. Beside her on her left lay the skeletal remains of a body. Based on the clothing - red shirt, white cardigan, plaid skirt - it was the woman Jamie saw in her vision, the one Isabelle Unger killed. *How are her remains still here?* Jamie thought. Then, she recalled that authorities removed thirteen bodies from the premises, including Isabelle's. Because they only found twelve victims, the police believed one person had escaped Reaper House and Isabelle's killing spree, though they never had anyone contact them to confirm. Even the police never discovered the secret room in the wall.

Downstairs, Pierce swallowed heavily at the masked figure's demand. He looked behind him and up to the second floor to see that Jamie was gone. He hoped she'd found a safe place to hide.

"I'm not fucking around anymore, Pierce," the voice behind the door barked. "Open the door!"

With worry on his face, Pierce pushed himself away from the door and unlocked the deadbolt. He backed away, almost tripping on Vickie's covered body. The doorknob slowly turned, and the door swung open, revealing the threatening figure. He wore the same white mask and white coveralls as the other two attackers, and he held a long machete in his right hand that was slung down by his side. He stepped through the door into the foyer, his dirty work boots scraping sand and gravel into the hardwood. He breathed heavily behind the mask and stared at Pierce, his eyes showing anger.

The figure looked down at the floor to his right at the body of the first masked man and huffed, shaking his head.

"What the fuck did you do?" he asked in a menacing voice.

Pierce looked worried and stuttered his response. "H-he...he fell down the stairs."

"He fell down the stairs," the masked man repeated calmly, unconvinced by Pierce's answer. Then his voice rose, "He fell down the fucking stairs?" The man ripped off his mask and charged at Pierce without Pierce making a move. The man grabbed the back of Pierce's neck and pulled him forward aggressively, stepping over the first dead man and marching into the library's doorway.

"And what about him?" The man asked. "Did he fall down the fucking stairs too?"

"N-no."

"Then I ask again, what the fuck did you do?"

"This one nearly beat the shit out of me," Pierce replied. "He didn't give me much choice. I was only defending myself. Fuck!"

"You do look a little banged up, don't you?"

"It wasn't supposed to be like this. You never said anything about killing anybody."

"So the boys got a little rambunctious. So what?"

"*So what?*" Pierce repeated angrily. "They were my friends."

"Three million dollars can *buy* you more friends," the man said with a smile.

"You're unbelievable, you know that? Who the hell were these guys, anyway? You didn't tell me you were bringing anyone else in."

The man pointed his machete into the foyer. "That one there is Brody Kiniely. You remember him, don't you?"

"Brody? Fuck. I haven't seen him since we were kids."

"This one's his younger brother." The man pointed the machete at the masked man in the library.

"That's little Charley?"

"Only he wasn't so little anymore. Shit! I'm going to have to break the news to their mother. Nice job, asshole. Now we're going to have to throw money her way to keep her from talking. That's coming out of *your* share."

The man looked to his left around Pierce, spying up the staircase curiously, and then to his right to scope out the library.

"So, where is she? The girl."

"She's not part of this," Pierce answered. "Just let her be."

The man squinted, fire in his eyes. He raised his arm in front of him and rammed it into Pierce's chest, driving him backward into the library's door jamb. "You think this is some sort of game, cous'?" he seethed through gritted teeth, spit flying from his lips. "You think we can just let her walk away after everything she's seen? After what we've done? Ain't no amount of money gonna keep her from yapping."

"She won't talk," Pierce said. "I'll make sure of that. Besides, she helped us out. She found it, man. She found where the old lady stashed the money."

"You're kidding me?"

"No. There's a hidden basement. It's filled with all kinds of boxes. I didn't get a chance to go through them, with everybody being here, but the money's got to be down there."

"Then, why are you still up here with me?" the man questioned, releasing his forearm from Pierce's chest. "Go get the money."

"Aren't you coming?" Pierce asked.

The man smiled deviously while looking up the staircase. "Nah, I think I'll wait right here for that pretty little girl of yours to show her face."

"Hey!" Pierce said sternly, staring the man down. "I told you, she's not part of this."

"I don't care what you said; she's gotta go."

The man wasn't backing down, and Pierce knew it. He stared at him intensely, his nostrils flaring with every breath.

"Fine," Pierce conceded. "But right now, she's upstairs hiding somewhere, and she's not about to come out anytime soon. We can deal with her after we have the money. I'm telling you, there are a lot of boxes down there; it'll go faster with both of us looking."

The man gave Pierce an annoyed look, then glanced back up the staircase. He exhaled through his nose.

"Fine. But you'd better be right about the money. *Your* ass is on the line, too."

Pierce simply nodded.

"Now, where is this secret basement you're talking about?"

"It's right in here," Pierce replied, backing up into the library. "Jamie found a hidden switch after I pulled a book from one of the shelves."

Pierce walked over to the far wall, where a vacant spot on the bookshelf still resided. He slid his hand sideways into the opening and hit the rocker switch. The shelf along the rear wall clicked open."

"You're shitting me?" The man said. "Like in the goddamn movies. This place is something else."

Pierce pulled the bookshelf open to reveal the stone steps leading down.

"Fuck me!" the man said. "That's creepy as shit."

"It's not that bad," Pierce responded.

The man waved his empty hand forward. "Then, by all means, after you, hotshot."

Chapter 37

It was dry and dusty in the claustrophobic space, but at least the rotting smell of the decomposing corpse had long since dissipated. Jamie thought of the vision she'd seen of Isabelle Unger killing this poor woman, snapping her neck, and dragging her dead body into this hidden crawlspace. It wasn't just a crazy daydream her mind had conjured. She wasn't unstable, reverting to her former self. It was all true. And if it was, what of the other visions she'd had?

She thought she was going crazy, seeing ghosts of dead people lurking within the mansion's eerie walls, but now she wasn't so sure. Those years in the institution taught her to differentiate what was real and what was only a figment of her distressed imagination. Her parents, her brother – they were dead; she knew that. She had stopped seeing them during her hospital stay, and they hadn't returned since. But this, what she was encountering within Reaper House, this was somehow real.

She lifted her palm from the dust-covered floor and brushed away the grit that had mingled with the blood she'd wiped from her head. The cut on her finger had already stopped bleeding, but she knew that wasn't the case with the large gash in her head. She could still feel the warm liquid seeping into her hair and brushing against the back of her neck.

She brushed her hands on her pants to clear them of any remaining debris while she stared at the skeleton beside her. Who was she? Did she have family? Did anyone report her missing? Did anyone even know she had gone to Reaper House that night? Were there people out there still wondering if she would ever come home? Or was she like Jamie, and had nobody left who would even notice she was gone?

She looked at the woman's stained clothing, darkened by the weeks and months she lay undisturbed, while her body slowly turned to liquid and melted away. The thought made Jamie queasy. She noticed a small, tan leather purse sandwiched between the wall and the woman's remains, the strap partially buried under the cardigan sweater she wore. Careful not to touch the skeleton, Jamie reached over and grabbed the purse. She unzipped the single pocket and rummaged through the contents: a pack of cigarettes, a lighter, a few folded receipts, an almost-empty pack of fresh mint Tic Tacs, a stick of ChapStick, a couple of credit cards, and finally, what Jamie was searching for, an ID.

She pulled the plastic card from the purse and read the name and address. Irina Stravenchuk, Carmella Way, Bristol, CT.

Jamie let out a sigh, feeling for the woman. It somehow felt more depressing knowing her name. She tucked the ID into her back pocket, zipped the purse back up, and tossed it back to its original spot by the wall. She was determined to get out of this nightmare situation, and when she did, she would make sure that whatever family or friends the woman had would finally receive closure.

Not knowing how long she would have to remain in her new temporary home, Jamie shifted around to get a sense of her surroundings. There wasn't a lot of space to maneuver, especially if she wanted to avoid touching the skeletal remains. Turning her head over her shoulder, she could see the space went back a significant distance. She slid herself on her butt until she was past the woman and able to rotate around.

Toward the back of the confined space, against both side walls, were four large, wooden rectangular trunks. Jamie tucked her legs under her until she was on her knees. A sharp pain caused her to wince, reminding her why that wasn't such a good idea. She raised her injured knee off the floor, digging the ball of her foot in instead, and keeping her weight on her one good knee. She crawled forward until she was between the four trunks. She flipped back over onto her butt and sat up, looking at the first trunk on her right. She imagined the worst: bones of past victims never found, tucked neatly away in a disturbed couple's hidden cubby, like a serial killer's prized possessions. She took a deep breath, let it out, and carried her trembling palm to the front of the trunk's cover. She sat frozen, running different scenarios in her mind, until she rationalized that pulling the band-aid off quickly was the best choice. Her arm tightened, and she shoved the lid open. Her first reaction was a nervous flinch, as she prepared for something to jump out at her. Her second reaction was that of astonishment.

While holding the cover open with one hand, she reached in and pulled out a neatly-wrapped stack of one-hundred-dollar bills.

"Holy shit!" she murmured. She lifted more of the money to see below, but it was more of the same: stacks and stacks of wrapped bills. She lowered the lid and reached for the cover to the trunk on her left. Opening it, she discovered more money. Piles of bills wrapped in little bands of yellow-colored paper, each one labeled $10,000. *The insurance money,* she thought. *Isabelle kept it with her, after all.*

Jamie closed the second trunk and glanced at the remaining two. She didn't need to open them;

she knew what she'd find. Her thoughts jumped to the masked men, once again. She had to be right. They must have been after the money. They didn't know where it was, but now, she did. If it came to it, maybe she could use that to her advantage. *But how did they even know about the money at all,* Jamie thought.

Just then, footsteps on the balcony floor just outside her hidden space pulled her from her thoughts. Her eyes widened with fear, worried she'd been found. Her eyes shifted to the lit bulb. Anxiety overtook her that its glow might give away her location. She quietly shuffled forward, ignoring the pain in her leg, reached for the dangling string, and clicked the light off.

She listened intently to the footsteps as they scurried back and forth across the floor, almost aimlessly. She thought she heard a voice whisper her name before the footsteps loudly trampled down the stairs. Then it came to her. Darlene.

It was too late to do anything about it. If it *were* her friend, Darlene would have already put herself in danger by running downstairs. Jamie didn't know where Pierce was, or if he was even still alive, but the masked man was down there somewhere. She hoped her friend ran straight for the door as fast as she could and got out of this hellish place. Imagining anything else was too painful and made Jamie feel guilty for staying safe. She hoped that soon, she could get out too.

Chapter 38

The cardboard box crashed to the floor, spilling its contents of fake, silicone rubber appendages across the concrete, as the man in white's temper flared.

"What the fuck is this shit!" he screamed. "You told me the money was down here. It's nothing but a bunch of plastic toys and rubber props. Fuck!"

"I'm telling you," Pierce responded, trying to calm the man down, "it's down here. We've only gone through seven boxes. There's still an entire wall to go through."

"You honestly want me to believe that woman would have put all her money in cardboard boxes and stored it down here with all of this haunted house gimmicky shit? You must be some kind of stupid, cous'."

"I'm not stupid. We've already scoured this house once before and found nothing. Do you think the old hag had a secret entrance to a basement concealed in her library bookshelf, only to have a place to store trinkets and other useless junk? The money is down here. I know it is."

"Yeah, well, you haven't convinced me of that yet, and I'm not playing games with you."

"Hey, it was *you* who asked me to help you in the first place."

"And you should be thanking me," the man said. "You're getting a lot of money out of this deal."

"Don't you mean, I should be thanking your mom?" Pierce questioned. "She's the one who told you about the insurance policy."

"The benefits of working for an insurance company for thirty years. But don't get me started. I'm still upset with the bitch for not mentioning it sooner."

"Hey, that's my favorite aunt you're talking about. Plus, you wouldn't be here now if not for me, so you can thank me for sharing the info with you."

"Whatever makes you feel good. But, come on. My old lady knew the old Unger hag had three million dollars and never said anything about it for over ten years. And since everyone knew the Ungers never went to the bank, it must be stashed somewhere in this house. Shit, we could have been rich while you were still in high school. And then that other unfortunate situation would never have happened.”

“That 'unfortunate situation' is on *you*,” Pierce responded, opening another box.

“Bullshit,” the man barked back. “You were right there with me, cous’. I saw the smile on your face and that gleam in your eye. You try to hide it, but you’re a sick fuck, just like me. Always have been. Always will be.”

“Shut up and keep looking, would ya?”

The man let out a snicker. He turned to face the stack of boxes and then stopped, glancing to his right into the shadowy area behind the stone steps.

“You are marked.”

“What the hell?” The man mumbled. “Did you hear that?

“What are you talking about?” Pierce asked, rummaging through his latest box.

“I thought I heard something.”

“Yeah, okay. Sure.”

The man stared into the darkness, his curiosity building.

“It is time.”

“There it is again. You didn’t hear that?”

“Cut it out. You’re not scaring me.”

The man stepped forward toward the direction of the faint whisper.

“The reckoning is at hand.”

As the man stepped closer, he became silent. His eyes glossed over as he slid his foot forward.

"Come to me. It is time. You are mine."

"Hey, are you all right over there?" Pierce asked, looking at the man's back as he slogged forward toward the darkened corner.

"Closer. Closer. Take my hand. Join me."

"What the fuck, man?" Pierce said in frustration. "Is this your way of trying to get out of doing the work?"

He watched as his cousin extended his arm forward like he was reaching for something.

"Yes. Take my hand. Closer."

"What is wrong with you?" Pierce questioned, stomping over. "I'm talking to you." He placed his hand on the man's shoulder and physically turned him around. When he did, the man's irises, which were rolled up behind his eyelids, snapped back into place, and he erupted into a fit of coughing like he hadn't been breathing.

"Whoa! Take it easy. Are you all right?"

"Yeah. Yeah, I'm fine," the man said, wiping his lips of spit and composing himself.

"What was that all about?" Pierce asked.

"What?"

"What do you mean, 'What?'? That whole bit with you walking off."

"What the fuck are you talking about? I didn't..,"

"Jamie?" A voice from upstairs called out.

The two men looked up at the ceiling.

"Jamie, where are you?" a woman's voice called again.

"Shit, that's Darlene!" Pierce stated excitedly.

"There's another one?" The man yelled angrily. "You dumb son of a bitch. We've got to stop her."

He ran to his machete, which leaned against the concrete wall, while Pierce grabbed his chef's knife from atop one of the boxes. They sprinted up the slate steps, back into the library, and out into the foyer.

"Do you think she ran out?" Pierce asked.

"Not out the front door," the man responded. "It's still closed. She wouldn't have taken the time to close it behind her."

"The back door is busted open," Pierce said.

"I'll check out back," the man said. "You go upstairs and find the other one."

"But..,"

"No arguments!" the man hollered. "You get her, and you bring her down here. Do you understand?"

"Y-yeah."

"Good. Now go."

Chapter 39

The heavy footsteps gave him away long before his voice. Pierce trotted up the staircase, two at a time, showing off his athleticism. When he reached the top, he called out for her.

"Jamie! Where are you? It's Pierce."

She sat quietly in the dark, her legs curled up to her chest, rocking back and forth. She was uncertain of what to do. Was Pierce alone? Did he fight off the masked man with the machete? Was he in cahoots with him? She didn't know who she could trust. And what about Darlene? Jamie heard her run downstairs moments before. Was she safe? Was she dead?

"Jamie, it's okay," Pierce yelled again. "You can come out now."

His voice was farther away that time, and to her left. He was standing where the hallway split in each direction. Should she call out to him? If she gave away her position, would she be rescued? Or would she be the next victim?

She listened carefully, hearing the bedroom doors down the left hallway slam shut after Pierce inspected each room.

"Jamie, come out!" she heard him yell again as he streaked down the right hallway, opening and closing doors in his pursuit to locate her. And then, a few seconds later, there was only silence, except for the sound of her breathing.

Jamie slid her body forward, accidentally putting her hand on the skeleton's femur before pulling it away and shaking it feverishly. She placed her ear to the door panel and listened. Even though the room was pitch black, her eyes darted in all directions. She was quiet. And she waited. And there was nothing, only stillness.

Like flashcards being displayed to her, her brain flipped through several scenarios, waiting for her to carry one of them out. One was to shuffle back and settle in for the night, hoping everyone would leave, and then she could come out of hiding when the coast was clear. But what of Darlene? What if she had a chance to save her friend but was too afraid to act? Another option was to get out of this enclosed hole in the wall right now. Her odds were at their best. If she was mistaken about Pierce, and there was no connection between him and the masked man, then there was a good chance he fought off the attacker. On the other hand, if they were working together, then the masked man was by himself on the first floor. Neither scenario was ideal, but she opted for the latter.

Breathing in and out to steady herself, she slid her hand along the wall until she found the button to open the door panel. She put her ear to the door one final time to ensure there was no sound. When she was satisfied, she pressed the button, and the panel slid open.

Light splashed across her face as she crawled out of the tight space, ignoring the pain in her knee. She looked toward the split hallways first, and then raised her head slightly to see through the balcony's balusters down to the first floor. Everything looked clear. She pressed the screwhead on the outlet and watched the wainscoting slide back into place.

Using the railing to support herself, Jamie hobbled forward to the staircase. Everything was still quiet. She knew she had to go now; Pierce would be coming back her way soon. She quietly limped down the stairs, sliding her arm along the banister, her eyes shifting from side to side, into the library, and then into the study, and back again. There was no movement. There was no sound. And the door was straight ahead of her. She could make it.

She stepped down off the last tread onto the foyer floor, placing her foot as lightly as possible between the dead man's legs to keep from making noise. Her other foot was going to be a struggle. She'd have to release the banister and put her full weight on her leg. She wasn't sure if she'd collapse, but she had to try. The door was only eight feet in front of her, and she was determined to make it. She clenched her teeth and pushed off the banister, stepping over the masked man's leg and placing the ball of her foot onto the floor. She felt the searing pain instantly, but hopped forward with her good leg to take the pressure off. She took another step. Then another. Then..,

"Well, hello there," the voice came from down the hallway behind her.

Jamie froze; her eyes flew open. She slowly turned her head to look over her shoulder as the man approached.

"We meet again," he said, as he grabbed a handful of hair and yanked her backwards. Jamie screamed as she stumbled over Vickie's body. Her foot caught on the blanket and pulled some of it away from the body, exposing her dead friend's arm and face. The man held her firm, dragging her to the entryway of the study, where he pulled her hair in a circle to spin her around to face him.

She gasped at the sight.

"You!"

"What's the matter, sweetheart, you don't like me anymore?"

She stared into the man's eyes as fear rolled up in her. Before she could react, he punched her in the face with the hand that held the machete, the blade nearly slicing her forehead. Blood spurted from her lips as she fell backward to the floor near the coffee table. She turned her face downward and watched a stream of blood leak from her mouth onto the floor. She spat to remove most of it from her tongue and looked up at the man who had hit her. It was the electrician who had turned on the power.

"Dave," she said, shaken and confused.

"Don't look so surprised," Dave said. "Who else do you think would have known you guys were up here? Shit, all of you being here gave us the perfect excuse to come back without worry of the police showing up."

"Us?" Jamie questioned. "The three of you fuckers?" *Eight plus three* still resounded in the recesses of her brain.

He flashed a maniacal grin. "Sure. Something like that."

Just then, Pierce came bounding down the stairs, shouting, "I can't find Jamie anywhere. I don't know where she..." He stopped at the base of the stairs when he saw her on the floor in the study. "Oh, fuck."

Jamie's lips quivered as she shook her head, her eyes welling up. She'd hoped it wasn't true, but now, there was no denying it.

Pierce stepped behind Dave, looking over his shoulder.

"*Us*," Dave repeated.

"Jamie, I'm so sorry," Pierce said. "I never meant for things to get this far."

"Shut up!" Jamie yelled.

"Hey, hey," Dave jumped in. "That's no way to talk to my cousin?"

"Your cousin?" Jamie questioned.

"On my mama's side," he nodded. "Hell, Pierce here is the one who tipped me off about you coming up here. After learning that, I volunteered for the meter job. We needed a reason to get back into this house. Pierce did the rest."

"*Back* into the house?"

"Oh, we've been here before, haven't we, Pierce?" He looked at Pierce over his shoulder.

"Knock it off," Pierce said. "Jamie, you have to..,"

"For the money, right?" Jamie quickly questioned, cutting off Pierce. "That's why you're here?"

"What the fuck?" Dave said, annoyed, turning around to look at Pierce. "You told her about the money?"

"N-no!" Pierce blurted nervously. "She said she read about it in a book."

"A book, huh?"

"Yeah. The one from the library. That was how she found the secret door to the basement."

"The basement where you think the old lady stashed the money."

"Yeah."

Jamie began laughing, gaining Dave's attention. He spun around, irate.

"Is something funny?" He questioned.

"Yeah, that you two think the money is down in the basement."

"Oh yeah? And you don't think it is?"

"No," she replied, smiling. "I know it's not down there. It's upstairs."

"And how do you know that?" the electrician asked.

"Because I've seen it."

Dave smirked skeptically and glanced at his cousin. Pierce shrugged his shoulders.

"I can show you," Jamie said.

"Damn straight you can show us," Dave said, stepping forward and grabbing her wrist. He yanked her to her feet, and she let out a scream, though she was unsure if it was her leg or the way he wrenched her wrist that caused more pain.

"Hey, take it easy on her," Pierce said.

"You want to hold onto her? Be my guest."

Dave shoved her into Pierce's arms. Jamie shook herself free from his touch. "Let go of me."

"I won't hurt you, Jamie."

"You've already hurt me, fucker! Look around. Look at me. Try saying it again, more convincing this time, you lying piece of shit. You make me sick."

"When you love birds are through, can you get a move on?"

Jamie limped forward, steering around Vickie's body to the base of the stairs. She grabbed the post and hopped onto the first step, paused to catch herself, then hopped onto the next.

"Oh, for Christ's sake," Dave spat. "Will you grab her and help her up, already? We don't have all night."

Like an obedient child, Pierce jumped into action, grabbing under Jamie's shoulder to help her along. Jamie pulled her arm away. "I can get there myself," she said through gritted teeth.

"Hey!" Dave yelled, placing the flat of the machete blade on Jamie's shoulder as a warning. "Let him help you."

Jamie huffed, having been given little choice. Pierce grabbed under her arm again, gentler this time, and eased her up the stairs. Once at the top, Jamie stopped.

"Where to now?" Dave questioned.

Jamie wiped her mouth of the blood and dragged her tongue across a cut on her lower lip.

"You've gotta promise to let me go," she said.

"And why would I do that? So you can go running off to the police?"

"I'm not gonna go to the police."

"Ha! You expect me to believe that shit?"

"I'm not gonna go to the police, because you're going to give me a cut of the money to ensure that I don't."

"Is that right?"

"Or, I don't show you where it is, and you'll never find it. Go ahead; kill me now and we all lose out, dumbfuck."

Dave smirked, shifting his eyes between Pierce and Jamie. "You didn't tell me she was as twisted as you. You know what? I'm nothing if not a generous man. You've got a deal. Money for your freedom. Lead the way."

"We're already here," she said.

The two men looked around, confused.

"Where is it? In the bathroom?" Dave asked.

Jamie didn't answer, only shook her head. She limped over to the wall across from the bathroom, bent down, and pressed the screwhead in the outlet. The wainscoting panel clicked and slid open, revealing the dark space.

"Well, look at that shit," Dave said. "This place has all kinds of secrets."

"It's in there," Jamie said.

Dave stepped to the opening and crouched down, looking into the darkness.

"How the fuck did you see anything in there?"

There's a pull switch in there for the light."

Dave turned to Pierce, "Get in there and check it out."

"Why me?"

"Because I don't trust your little girlfriend here. Now find the switch and turn on the light."

Pierce exhaled in frustration and crouched by the entrance. "A pull switch?" he questioned.

"A few feet in," Jamie replied. "When you get in there, wave your arm around, you'll feel it."

Pierce stepped into the darkness and threw his arm forward, wagging it from side to side, until a smile came to his lips. He pulled the string, and the space lit up. He immediately threw himself backward at the sight of the skeletal remains.

"Holy shit! Fuck! Why didn't you warn me about that?"

"Oops, I guess I forgot."

Pierce composed himself and squatted in the opening again.

"The money's in the trunks in the back," Jamie said.

Dave forced himself forward and shoved his cousin aside to look into the confined space. He smiled from ear to ear at the sight of the trunks. "Well, let's see what we have there." He squeezed himself through the opening and shimmied to the back. The bulb immediately flickered, catching his attention. He then noticed a temperature shift; his breath became visible as he exhaled. "Holy shit, it's cold in here," he said. The light flickered again.

"I guess your electrical skills need a little work," Pierce jabbed.

"That's not my electrical skills, asshole. It's probably a bad bulb."

He placed the machete on the floor by his feet and grabbed the first trunk's lid. When he opened it, his face lit up brighter than the bulb. He turned to look out at Pierce. "We're fucking rich!"

Just as the words left his lips, the panel door slid closed, sealing him inside. Jamie shuffled back in shock. Dave began screaming, "Hey, open the damn door."

"What did you do?" Pierce yelled. "Open the door!"

"I didn't do anything," Jamie answered.

Pierce pushed Jamie out of the way and pressed the screwhead on the outlet, but nothing happened. Dave began pounding his fists on the interior of the door, screaming to be let out, and threatening to kill them if they didn't.

"What the hell, Jamie? Why isn't it opening?"

"I don't know."

Pierce continued to press the button while Dave yelled obscenities until suddenly, the yelling stopped.

"Dave?" Pierce called through the panel.

And then, as quickly as it had stopped, the screams began again, only this time, it was an awful shrieking sound that could cut into a person's soul, like a banshee's wail. Pierce backed away from the wall, fearing something would come through.

"What the fuck is happening?" he questioned as Dave's horrific screams continued.

Jamie's eyes remained wide as she slowly backed away toward the staircase. She didn't know what was happening, but with Pierce distracted, this was her chance to get away. She shambled onto the stairs and forced herself down, feeling every ounce of pain when she put any amount of weight on her leg.

"Dave!" Pierce yelled, even as Dave's howls drowned him out.

Jamie continued her struggle one step at a time, with tears forming in her eyes. And then, the awful screaming ended. She turned her body slightly to look up toward the balcony and lost her grip on the banister. She fell sideways, tumbling down the rest of the stairs until she came to a stop at the bottom, hitting the back of her head once again. She tried to focus as everything became fuzzy, but the blurry shape of a man, standing at the top of the staircase, was all she needed to see. Pierce was coming.

Chapter 40

She pushed herself up onto her elbows, shaking her head to rid herself of the haze. She glanced up and saw Pierce slowly walking down the stairs; the hand he held the knife in was twitching. From his appearance, he wasn't happy.

Jamie kicked her legs, pushing herself off the dead masked man's body. Every part of her was aching, and her head was throbbing. She could feel more of the warm liquid trickling out of the gash, coloring her hair a redish-brown.

"What did you do to him?" Pierce seethed, making his way down the stairs.

Jamie tried pleading with him as she maintained her struggle to crawl away. "That wasn't me. I have no idea what happened." Her words came out shaky and labored, as it hurt to breathe. She kept her eyes on Pierce's progress. He took his time descending the staircase. He knew there was nowhere for her to go, and she couldn't run if she tried.

"You lie!" he shouted. "You tricked him into going in there."

"I didn't," Jamie replied. She dug her heels into the hardwood and pushed with all her might, her leg screaming at her to give in, but she wouldn't.

"What was it, Jamie? Knives coming out of the walls? Was the floor wired? Was he electrocuted? What was it? What was in there?"

Jamie shook her head. "I don't know. I don't know what that was."

"Why are you lying to me?"

"I'm not," she answered, pushing herself through the study's doorway as Pierce reached the foyer floor. "It's this house."

"Just tell me... is he dead?"

Jamie pursed her lips and shook her head. "I don't know."

"God, why are you doing this?" Pierce shouted. "I didn't want this to happen. I was trying to save you." Pierce stopped under the arched doorway.

Jamie continued to push herself on her butt farther into the room.

"I was going to make a life for us," Pierce continued. "That's what the money was for. I didn't know they were going to kill our friends."

"What the hell did you think was going to happen?" she questioned.

"He said he was going to scare you all away. It's a freaking haunted house. I didn't know he was going to bring the other two in."

The words from the book popped into Jamie's head. *The two had returned, and in doing so, had sealed their fate.*

"How did everything become such a mess?" he asked, rhetorically. "Chuck, Shawn, Samara, Vickie... they were my friends."

"Ha! Your friends," Jamie said. "Good one. And what about Brandon?" Jamie added. "That was you, wasn't it? You killed him."

"I couldn't let him leave," Pierce admitted. "He was going to bring back others. That would have ruined everything."

"So, you killed him?" Jamie yelled.

"Come on, we didn't even really like him."

"You're crazy."

"No. No, I'm not. Of the two of us, who's been locked in an institution for seeing ghosts?"

"That's not fair," Jamie retorted, pushing herself past the coffee table.

"Not fair?" Pierce responded. "It's your fault I'm even involved in all of this."

Jamie shook her head, confused. "My fault? How is any of this my fault?"

"You were in the hospital when my cousin first asked if I'd help him a few years back. If you hadn't been away, I never would have agreed to it. But I didn't have anything else."

"You're delusional."

"I told you, I'm not!" Pierce said heatedly, gripping the knife tighter. "All of this, what's happened here, it's all on you. It's your boss who bought the place. You invited us all here to help you out. You called for an electrician to turn the power on. If not for you, this never would have happened. Our friends would still be alive."

"You're a fucking psycho, you know that? I can't believe I ever had feelings for you. But you know what I don't understand? Why wait until now?" Jamie questioned. "Dave said you were both here before, looking for the money. Why hadn't you been looking for it that whole time?"

"We couldn't. After what happened the first time..." He dropped his chin to his chest. "After that, the police randomly patrolled the mansion."

"Why? What happened the first time?"

Pierce remained silent, shaking his head.

"Pierce," Jamie insisted. "What happened?"

He looked at her with sullen eyes, exhaling heavily through his nose.

"They weren't supposed to be here. We didn't even hear them come in."

"Who?"

"You know who. The brothers. You saw their graves out back."

"Thomas and Rory Wilkinson," Jamie whispered, her eyes flaring open. "Oh my God!" She brought her hand to her mouth.

"That fucking older boy couldn't keep his mouth shut, threatening to tell his uncle we were there looking for money. He didn't know me, since I'm from out of state, but everybody around here knows my cousin. Even after Dave threatened him, he still said he was going to do it. Then, the kid said, if we didn't find the money, he and his brother would be back to look for it. That made Dave furious. He ran out of the house and to his truck. A minute later, he came back with some rope. He grabbed the younger boy and dragged him upstairs. The older brother chased after them, punching at Dave, but Dave just brushed him off like it was nothing. I thought he was joking, you know, to get his point across. He threw the handful of rope over the balcony onto the chandelier, holding onto one end. He wrapped it around the boy's neck four or five times. I yelled up to him. 'Come on, Dave. Enough is enough. Joke's over.' The older brother was kicking and screaming. Dave shoved him away. And then, before I knew it, he threw the younger brother over the balcony. The pile of rope caught on the chandelier, and it was done. The boy was dead. Dangling there. Snapped neck.

"I couldn't believe what had just happened. I was in shock. The older brother ran down the stairs past me, heading for the back door. Dave yelled down to me. 'Don't just stand there, idiot. Do you want to go to prison? Get him.'

"I still don't know why I listened to him. Everything was happening so fast. Things weren't registering. I chased after the boy. He ran out the back door and through the cemetery. There was a rusty machete leaning against the house outside the back door. I don't even remember grabbing it. I don't remember much of anything except standing over his body in that field out back, the machete dripping with blood."

"You killed those boys," Jamie said softly.

Just then, the lamp in the study began to flicker, and the temperature dropped.

Pierce continued. "Dave got the step ladder from his truck, climbed up to the younger brother's hanging body, and jabbed a knife into his chest with a note attached to it."

"The reaper made me do it," Jamie said.

Pierce looked at her, perplexed. "Yeah. How did you..,"

The lamp dimmed slowly and then brightened to a blinding level. Jamie and Pierce turned their heads away. Then it dimmed again to its normal brightness before flickering on and off rapidly.

"What the hell is going on?" Pierce said, stepping forward.

Jamie pointed at him, "Stay the fuck away from me."

"I can't, Jamie. I love you. Can't you see that?"

Jamie looked around her in a panic. To her left, sitting on the end table, was the silicone arm

Pierce had taken from his room, beside it, the rubber knife. She reached over and grabbed the knife, then pointed it at Pierce threateningly.

"I said, stay the fuck away from me." Her breath exited her mouth in a plume of condensation in the chilled air. "*You* did all of this. You and your fucking cousin. You killed those two boys. And then you came back to cause more misery and pain. I get it now."

"Get *what* now?"

"*The two had returned, and in doing so, had sealed their fate.*"

"What the hell are you blathering on about?"

"You're dead," Jamie yelled. "You hear me? You're fucking dead." She slashed the rubber knife in the air threateningly in front of her.

"Do you really think you're going to kill me with that rubber knife?"

Jamie stopped waving the prop around and looked him in the eyes. "Not *this* knife."

Before Pierce could move, something from behind him gripped him tightly and held him fast. Darlene popped up over his shoulder, her eyes solid black, holding the knife she'd removed from Vickie's chest. She held the knife to Pierce's throat and stared across the room at Jamie. In a guttural voice, she spoke, "The reaper comes for us all." With a jerk of her wrist, steel sliced through skin and cartilage. It was done. Pierce's throat had been slashed. Blood spilled out onto his clothes and the hardwood. His body convulsed before crumpling to the floor.

Darlene stood for a moment longer, possessed of whatever was inside her, and then her eyes reverted to normal, and she collapsed to the floor.

The words from the book rang in Jamie's head yet again. *The reaper had been summoned, once again, to take what was due. Vengeance will not rest until the last one has fallen.*

Ten minutes later, Darlene finally opened her eyes. Sitting over her, running her fingers through her hair, was Jamie.

"Hey," Jamie said softly, smiling. "How are you feeling?"

"Wh-what happened?"

"It's all over. We're safe."

Darlene turned her head slightly to see Pierce, lying in a pool of his blood. She shot up to a sitting position.

"What the Fuck? What the fuck?"

"Don't you dare cry for him," Jamie said. "He did this. He did all of this. He killed our friends."

"What? Pierce?"

Jamie nodded. "Can you get up?"

"I-I think so." She pushed herself up to her feet.

"Good. Now you can help me up." She extended her arm. Darlene latched onto it and pulled her up, holding onto her so she wouldn't fall backward. "Let's get outta here."

They supported each other as they staggered to the front door. Stepping out onto the porch, Jamie heard her phone beep. She pulled it out of her pocket and looked at the screen, fully lit and with full service.

"Well, look at that," Jamie said, handing it to Darlene. "You sit here and call the police. I'll be right back."

Darlene sat on the top step and dialed 911, while Jamie hobbled her way back into the mansion. She glanced into the study and saw the book on the floor between the sofa and coffee table. Her body numb with shock, she limped into the study and picked up the book, then made her way across the foyer to the library, where she flipped through the pages. It didn't surprise her to see that they were all blank. She placed the book back in its rightful spot.

Shambling back into the foyer, she stopped, looked down the hallway toward the kitchen, then shifted her eyes up the staircase and smiled devilishly.

Ten minutes later, Jamie emerged from the mansion's front door carrying four reusable grocery bags. She tottered down the porch steps past Darlene to her vehicle. She opened the trunk, placed the bags inside, and closed the lid.

Hearing sirens in the distance, Jamie hobbled her way back to Darlene and sat beside her, staring down the long driveway to where it disappeared around a bend.

"You think we'll get out of here tonight?" Jamie asked.

Darlene looked at the phone and flashed the time to Jamie. "You mean this morning? What was that, anyway?" Darlene asked, nodding to the car.

"Nothing," Jamie replied. "I didn't want to leave without my dishes."

Epilogue

Sitting in her favorite lounge chair on her back deck, Jamie admired the ocean's waves as high tide swept in. She loved the smell of the salty air as the breeze crested off the sandy dunes. It had been just over a year since she quit her job at Blanchard Realty Investments and left her former life behind. There was nothing left for her back there save Darlene, and even Darlene became more and more distant after the traumatizing events of those two days at Reaper House. Jamie packed her things and moved to a tranquil locale, settling into a small cottage on a beach in Cape Cod, Massachusetts. It was close enough for the occasional visits with her friend, but far enough away from that disturbing mansion, though she still had nightmares of the horror she lived through.

The thought of that place gave her chills as she sipped on her strawberry margarita. She hadn't cared to stick around long enough to find out if her former boss followed through with updating and reselling the property. She was content with spending her peaceful days and calm nights in the comfort of her little beachhouse, taking frequent trips into town to visit the quaint shops and local eateries. She quickly realized she could spend hours listening to the waves roll in. Even as the evenings became brisk, it was still her happy place. So much happier than the horrifying scene she'd left behind.

She recalled her and Darlene's last evening at that dreaded house; they'd lost all their friends. Darlene struggled with remembering most of the events of that night, and she was better off for it. Knowing all the gruesome details was Jamie's burden. Jamie left with a concussion from her head injury, which required twelve stitches. She still considered herself fortunate to be alive. Especially after what she'd seen when she went back upstairs. She replayed it over again in her head many nights.

Jamie shambled back into the foyer. She stopped, looked down the hallway toward the kitchen, then shifted her eyes up the staircase, and smiled devilishly. She knew what she had to do.

She limped down the hallway as quickly as her leg would allow, steering clear of the drops of blood leading into the bedroom beyond the staircase, where Shawn had been horrifically slain. She entered the kitchen, and on the counter beside the refrigerator, grabbed the reusable shopping bags they'd brought with them. She scrambled back down the hallway toward the front door, picking up her pace. She told Darlene to call the police; she had to act quickly. She scuttled up the stairs, using the banister to pull herself up. When she got to the top, she paused to quickly pay her respects to Samara. She hobbled to the side wall, pressed the button in the center of the outlet, and watched the wainscoting panel slide open. The moment Darlene had taken Pierce's life and collapsed, Jamie knew there was nothing more to be afraid of. The Reaper had served its vengeance against the men who had ruthlessly killed the Wilkinson brothers. There was nothing more to fear. But there was still a mess Jamie had to conquer.

Inside the small cubby where Dave the electrician had gotten trapped, something had torn him apart. The light was still on, and Jamie had a clear view of the horror. The floor, walls, and ceiling of the confined space were painted with his blood, his flesh ripped from his bones in chunks and splattered around the small space. He had *gotten what was coming to him and exactly what he deserved.*

Jamie gathered her courage, placed one hand under her nose to try to minimize the awful smell of blood and organ waste, and stepped inside. She squeezed her way past Irina's bones and the unrecognizable remains of what used to be Dave. She opened the first trunk and began filling the grocery bags with the stacks of one-hundred-dollar bills until the chest was empty. She opened the second trunk and filled the remaining bags. She closed the trunks, setting them back as they were, and made her way back out of the small room, turning the light off as she left. She pressed the button on the outlet to close the panel door and seal the room's secrets once more. Then she made her way back down the stairs hastily and out the door.

Two days later, she traveled to Bristol, Connecticut, to deliver the news to Irina's family. The woman's father had since passed away. Her mother was still in the same house, though she was disabled. Irina's brother had moved back in to care for her. Jamie didn't tell them everything, only that Irina's remains had been discovered and that she had been one of the victims of Isabelle Unger. She left them with one of the grocery bags of money. It couldn't bring Irina back, but she hoped it could provide financial comfort.

She was proud of herself for what she'd done. When she returned, she visited Darlene and left her with a second bag of cash. She'd kept enough money for herself, too. And why not? She'd been through hell and back. Why shouldn't she be able to enjoy herself? One point four million dollars can go a long way.

She took another sip of her drink and smiled. She got up from her chair and walked through the rear door of her house. She was getting hungry and decided it was time to take a trip into town for dinner. She placed her glass in the sink and swiped the keys to her Porsche from the counter. As she headed for the front door, she stopped and stared at the couch in her living room, making a funny face.

"No, Mom. I'm just going out to grab a bite to eat. I won't be long." Her eyes shifted slightly to the other side of the couch. "Okay, Dad, I'll drive carefully." Finally, she glanced at an empty chair and rolled her eyes. "Fine, you can come with me, Trevor, as long as you behave."

She opened the front door and waited, gesturing for her brother to step through. Then, she turned to face the empty living room and said, "Be back soon; love you both," before stepping out and closing the door behind her.

A LETTER FROM THE AUTHOR

Dear readers,

I hope you loved *Reaper House*. A fan had suggested I write a book about a haunted house to see how it would compare to others they'd read. I thought it was a great idea, since I hadn't written one before. I wanted it to have a different feel than your ordinary haunted house tale, and I hope I managed to pull it off.

If you think I did, and if you enjoyed the story, I'd be very grateful if you'd consider writing a review. I love to hear what readers think, which only helps me grow as an author, and it makes such a difference in helping new readers discover my books for the first time.

While you're at it, check out my website at:

javo-publication.square.site

Where copies of all of my books (including signed copies) can be purchased. You can also find them on Amazon or ask your local bookstore to order them.

Thank you so much for your kind support!
Jeff

Acknowledgments

I sound like a broken record when I thank my editor, Elizabeth Kelly, but she absolutely leads me in the right direction with her subjective comments and suggestions. All of my books have gotten better because of her guidance and detail.

Thank you to Loni Pysz for being a beta reader for this book and giving it to me straight when you felt a chapter needed reworking.

I want to thank the members of the WhipCity Wordsmiths, whose support and honest feedback are so greatly appreciated during my writing process. They helped me resolve a few issues in the opening chapters of this book.

Thank you, Mark Jenkins, Kristi Guthrie, and Billie Jean Wiley for allowing me into your groups and being supportive of authors such as myself. It means a lot to those of us still trying to get our books in the hands of readers.

It wouldn't be right if I didn't acknowledge those who have offered such wonderful support: Jamie Smith, Sorell Locke, Fabian Harmsen, Brandy D. Osborn, Tracy Hinson, Tara Leigh, Andrew Baumgardner and so many others. If I didn't catch you this time, I'll get you on the next.

Thank you all.

On to the next.

Jeff VanOudenhove has written several novels in the genre of dark fiction, including the **Dark Series,** a psychological thriller with supernatural elements, crime thrillers **The Alphabet Killer, The Letter Man**, and **Killer By Number,** the psychological suspense thrillers **Just Listen** and **Emma**, and a book of truly twisted short stories, **Screams in the Dark and Other Twisted Tales**. His talent for storytelling combines unforgettable characters and dire situations, mixed with astonishing plot twists. **Reaper House** is Jeff's twelfth book. He lives in Western Massachusetts with his wife, Elena.